Animal
Attraction

How Not to Spend Your Senior Year
BY CAMERON DOKEY

Royally Jacked
BY NIKI BURNHAM

Ripped at the Seams
BY NANCY KRULIK

Spin Control
BY NIKI BURNHAM

Cupidity
BY CAROLINE GOODE

South Beach Sizzle
BY SUZANNE WEYN AND DIANA GONZALEZ

She's Got the Beat
BY NANCY KRULIK

30 Guys in 30 Days
BY MICOL OSTOW

A Novel Idea
BY AIMEE FRIEDMAN

Animal Attraction

JAMIE PONTI

Simon Pulse
New York London Toronto Sydney

SIMON PULSE
An imprint of Simon & Schuster
Children's Publishing Division
1230 Avenue of the Americas, New York, NY 10020
Copyright © 2005 by James Ponti

SIMON PULSE and colophon are registered trademarks of Simon & Schuster, Inc.

Designed by Ann Zeak
The text of this book was set in Garamond 3.

Manufactured in the United States of America
First Simon Pulse edition August 2005

10 9 8 7 6 5 4 3 2 1
Library of Congress Control Number 2005927084
ISBN 1-4169-0987-7

For Denise

Acknowledgments

For expertise in the worlds of high school and swimming, I am deeply indebted to Kevin Latham, Patty Worsham, Rob Quel and the pit bulls of E.C. Glass. Likewise, I would have been lost without the help of my teen consultant Virginia Gray Bailey.

I received invaluable feedback and support from Catherine Snowden, Trish Bartholomew, and Julie Komorn. I also had the great joy of working with the incomparable Michelle Nagler and Bethany Buck, who oddly enough returned my calls.

Most of all, I'd like to thank my family, especially the real Alex and Grayson.

One

I am the victim of a global conspiracy.

I know that sounds overly dramatic—like one of those *Everwood* episodes where Ephram and Amy break up, get back together, and break up again all before the first commercial—but it's the only explanation I can think of.

For seventeen years my life has been just like those shows on the History Channel that my dad is always forcing me to sit through. (He loves to say, "Watch with me, Janey. It's like *The Real World*, only real.") Except unlike *The D-Day Conspiracy* or *The Pearl Harbor Conspiracy*, which only *seem* like they last forever, *The Jane Conspiracy* is endless.

Apparently, everyone on the freaking planet has plotted to make sure that I am never anywhere in the vicinity of being cool and that under no circumstance do I ever meet a boy.

I've got to hand it to them: Their record is spotless—so far.

But things are going to change. *This* summer is going to be different. I was inspired by an unlikely source: my big sister, Kendra. She's a junior at Florida State, and last month she came home for a three-day weekend to get her laundry done, sponge money off my parents, and hook up with her ex-boyfriend Erik. (Or, as she told Mom and Dad, "Because I missed you all so much.")

Somehow in the middle of all that manipulating, she actually found time to give me some good advice. (That's once in seventeen years, but she means well.)

"Make the most of this summer," she told me. "It should be the best three months of your life."

We were having a girls' day at the time. Mom had given us some money and the keys to her car, and told us to go have fun. (Mom is always trying to bring us closer together.) As we drove to the mall, Kendra explained the crucial nature of the summer before senior year.

"You're almost old enough to be an adult, but you don't have any adult responsibilities," she reasoned. "The summer after graduation will be all about getting ready for college. So *this* is the summer to really have fun!"

Normally, Kendra's idea of advice is something she read on an Abercrombie & Fitch T-shirt. So this was a big deal. For a second I even thought we were going to bond. But then she dumped me at the mall so she could go "bond" with Erik.

Still, it was a nice moment.

I kept thinking about it as I bought a jewel belt at the Gap. And I thought about it some more when I got some jeans on sale at Hollister. (I got all of the money in exchange for keeping quiet about Erik.)

In fact, the more I thought about it, the more I realized she was right. I had to make the most of this summer. I decided that it would mark the end of the conspiracy.

That night I was watching *Behind the*

Music on VH1. The show was about this old alt-rock group called the B-52's. They were hilarious with huge beehive hairdos and retro thrift store clothes. They sang this great song called "The Summer of Love." I instantly decided that it would become my new theme.

Now it's six weeks later and my plan is coming together. (I'm also wearing the jeans, which I love.) Today is the last day of school and I drove to campus in a brand-new, oh-so-adorable Cabriolet. Okay, technically it's nine years old, but it's brand-new to me.

Having a car changes everything. No more begging for rides. No more getting stuck at lame parties with no way home. And no more waiting in the mall parking lot while Kendra's off somewhere macking with Erik.

I am now 100 percent mobile Jane.

Of course, the car comes with a catch. I have to pay for half of it. The deal my parents gave me is that I give them the money—$1,250—by the end of summer. To do this, I have arranged for not one but two summer jobs.

For the third straight year, I'll be giving swimming lessons at the Y. Usually, I give group lessons, but now I'm going to do one-on-one. One-on-one's kind of tricky. The pay's better, but you can get stuck with a nightmare kid. For a car, though, it's totally worth the risk.

When I'm done at the pool, I will hop into my Cabrio—how I love to say that—and drive to job number two at Tragic Waters. (That's what the locals call Magic Waters.)

Magic Waters is a lame amusement/theme park that was a big deal back in the fifties. People actually used to come all the way to Florida just to see it. My heart aches for how starved for entertainment they must have been. To modern eyes, it's just a collection of dinky rides and mind-numbing shows like the Mermaid Spectacular.

The mermaid show is what made Magic Waters famous. Twice a day, tourists watch six girls wearing clamshell bikini tops and body fins perform underwater to music. It sounds pathetic (who am I kidding, it *is* pathetic), but it's got a kind of tacky kitsch appeal. There's also a huge upside for the mermaids—boys.

For thirty minutes after the show, the 'maids swim around the fake lagoon and pose for pictures. That's where the boys come in. Tons of them. By the early afternoon, most guys have decided that talking with a mer-chick in a bikini is a lot more fun than waiting in line to ride the Sea Serpent for the fourteenth time.

Here's the amazing part. This summer, I'm going to be one of the mer-chicks. (This and a car, it's like I'm moving from the History Channel to the WB.) Most 'maids are picked because they have C cups and perfect skin. I was picked for a different reason. I can swim circles around the other girls. In fact, that's literally what I do during the show's finale.

I'm the best swimmer at Ruby Beach High. Good enough that I'm hoping to snag a scholarship or at least make a top college swim team. The mermaid show needs at least one great swimmer for the tricky moves.

This year, it's me.

It doesn't matter if the other girls have better skin or bigger boobs. I'll be one of only six mermaids surrounded by dozens of boys on a daily basis. Not even a global conspiracy can overcome those odds.

I can't help but smile as a now familiar song plays in my head. It's the B-52's and they're singing away.

"It's the summer of love, love, love. . . ."

TWO

The smell of Sloppy Joes is so strong that I feel dizzy just walking past the cafeteria. The students aren't supposed to know that the lunch budget ran out three weeks ago. The school's gotten by with leftovers, and a large shipment of "alternate food product" that was purchased with an emergency loan from the PTA. (I was warned by my mom, who's an English teacher and a member of the PTA board.)

It's not like I needed the extra incentive to avoid the cafeteria. I always brown bag it and eat on the patio with my two best friends, Becca and Melanie. We started eating lunch together in the fourth grade, the year Becca's family moved here from Cuba.

We've been inseparable ever since, which is why they grant me all of three seconds to sit down before they launch into me.

"I can't believe you got a car and didn't tell us," Becca says between sips of her Diet Dr Pepper.

I plead for forgiveness. "I didn't know. My parents surprised me. I thought we were going to get it next weekend."

It's pointless to defend myself. They're not even listening.

"It's the mermaid thing," Melanie says with authority. "We're getting replaced by the C Cups."

This is officially Day Five of the Jane Abuse Tour.

Bec and Mel—my two oldest, dearest friends on the planet—have been giving me nonstop hell every day since I got the mermaid job. Like it's going to change me.

"I bet she told Crystal," Becca adds with a pointed look. "Mermaids share everything. It's part of their code."

Melanie nods in agreement as she chomps on a carrot stick. "Are you kidding?

She probably already gave Crystal a ride."

"Right," I answer, finally getting a word in. "She really wants to ride in my nine-year-old Volkswagen instead of the pimped out Beemer she got for her birthday."

This logic finally slows the assault.

Becca's the first to concede. "Okay. We went too far with that one."

"Yeah, I guess so," Melanie agrees. "I still can't believe her parents gave her such a sweet car. Life is just not fair."

"Just not fair" is often used to describe the charmed life of Crystal Gentry. The Queen Bee of Ruby Beach High, she's a third-year varsity cheerleader, a second-generation mermaid, and a first-degree bitch.

We also share a history.

There was a time when the three of us were the four of us. Crystal was the fourth. We hung together all through elementary and middle school. We were really tight. Then, when we got to high school, Crystal was gone. She joined the elites and she never looked back.

Becca flashes a sly smile. "Do you think the rumor's true? Do you think that in addition to the car, her parents also got her a boob job?"

This is the hottest gossip at school. I don't think it's true, but I don't disagree when anyone says it. I don't know if that makes me a bad person or anything. I just don't like her.

Crystal and I have been enemies ever since she ditched the group. The problem is that now we'll also be coworkers. When I got the mermaid job, the two of us kind of agreed to a truce for the summer. Bec and Mel still haven't forgiven me for that.

"Just promise that you won't dump us for her," Melanie says, joking, but maybe a little bit serious. "Fake or real, those things attract a lot of boys, and you might be tempted to hang around for the overflow."

"I promise—again," I say strong enough so she knows I mean it. "And that's why I want you two to be the first ones to ride in my new car. I'll drive us all to the park for the ritual."

They share a disapproving look.

"Sorry, can't make it," Becca says.

"Yeah," Mel adds. "Sorry."

"What do you mean?" I say, not believing

this. "Today's the last day of school! It's our tradition!"

"Yeah," Becca says. "But Crystal wants to be friends again and she offered to give us a ride in the Beemer."

Melanie shrugs. "Although we're stuck with our original boobs."

With that, we all laugh, which feels good. Things have been tense lately, and I guess I understand. The three of us have mocked the mermaids for as long as I can remember. And I do feel a little bad about it. Because maybe all that mocking was really jealousy. Now that I'm one, I'm really excited. Maybe they're jealous of me. But no one could ever replace Bec and Mel. They must know that.

"Quincy!" The name echoes across the patio attracting far more attention than I'd like. I turn and see Coach Latham, my swim coach and the only person on earth who calls me by my last name. I smile and wave, hoping he will quiet down.

"My office!" he barks before disappearing back into the physical education building.

Becca laughs. "You've got to give him

credit. He does not waste a lot of time with extra words."

"I've studied it," Melanie comments. "His trick is that he doesn't use verbs. Can you imagine how he proposed to his wife? 'Marriage! You and me!'"

I quickly gather my stuff and turn to them. "After school. In the parking lot."

"She's the same way. No verbs. Must be a swim thing."

I roll my eyes and rush over to the office. Coach Latham does not like to wait. I bet he wants to go over my summer workout schedule. He's always worried that we'll party too much and get out of shape. Personally, that's what I'm shooting for.

"Quincy, it's a good thing you swim faster than you run," he says as I hurry into the room.

"I had to get my books," I explain. Then he looks up and I realize he's only joking.

"Sit down, we need to talk."

Suddenly, this sounds serious.

Despite his gruff, verb-free exterior, Coach Latham is a total teddy bear. He coaches both the boys' and girls' swim teams and even drives the bus to meets. (He started doing this when he learned the bus driver was making more money than he was for coaching.) He's also been trying to help me land a scholarship.

He hands me an envelope. It's a recruiting letter from the University of Southern California. My heart skips a beat. USC is my first choice, and not just because it's in L.A., which would be awesome. Great school. Great swim team. Great everything.

"The coach was very interested when I told him about your times at state this year," he says.

I can't help but smile. For some unexpected reason I dominated at the state swim meet. I swam PRs—personal records—in my two main events. And, in a huge upset, I won the 200-yard IM (individual medley), touching the wall just ahead of a girl named Tina Sue Hinton, who got a full-ride scholarship to Stanford. I got my picture in the paper and everything. It was the closest to cool I'd ever been.

"But, he wants to make sure it wasn't a fluke," Coach Latham continues.

"Which means?"

"Which means," he says with a smile, "if you keep swimming like you did at state, I think they'll offer at least a partial athletic scholarship. With your grades, tack on an academic one and you'll be set."

I try to catch my breath. This is huge. We aren't exactly wealthy, and with Kendra still in college, money's tight at home. Landing a scholarship would be incredible.

"It also means," he says, bringing me back to earth, "that you're going to have to train your butt off this summer. Nothing's set, and there's a whole year left to screw things up."

He hands me a workout schedule. It's brutal. Two jobs and training my butt off—this should leave plenty of time for an active social life.

"Absolutely," I tell him, finally catching my breath.

I can hardly contain myself. First, the car. Then the mermaid show. Now this. It's as if seventeen years of nothing going right is all turning around in one week.

"Thanks," I say as I get up to go.

"Down," he says, signaling me to sit.

Then it happens.

The global conspiracy to keep me uncool and unattached rears its ugly head. He pulls out another envelope. This one is from the state athletic association.

"I've been reading over the new eligibility guidelines," he said. "And you're not going to be able to swim at Magic Waters this summer."

At first, I think he's joking, and I start to laugh.

"You're going to have to find a different job," he continues.

I'm still laughing, but I realize that he's not laughing with me. He's serious. "Why?" I ask.

He explains that a new rule was passed because some high school basketball star got paid tons of money to be in a movie. According to the rule, if I get paid to swim in a show, it would make me a professional swimmer. And professionals are ineligible to swim for their high school or college teams.

I just sit there for a moment and let it sink in.

Good-bye, mermaid show.

Good-bye, boys.

Good-bye, summer of love.

Three

By the end of the day, I'm completely mental. I'm excited about summer vacation, but pissed about the mermaid show. I can't believe that USC is interested in me, but I'm trying not to get my hopes up. I finally have a car, but now I don't know how I'll pay for it.

(It also officially marks another school year gone by without a significant boyfriend. Not that I'm keeping track or anything.)

Like I said—completely mental.

Since it's the last day of school, the student parking lot is even more of a zoo than usual. There are people everywhere, and someone is blasting 50 Cent so loud that the windows are about to vibrate out of his car.

I fight my way through a maze of people hugging, kissing, and making phony promises to keep in touch over the summer. Three sophomore girls are saying tearful good-byes to one another while a boy stares at them in total disbelief.

"Why are you crying?" he asks, dumbfounded. "You cry on the *first* day of school, not the *last*!"

When I finally make it through the crowds, I find Becca and Melanie leaning against my car with big goofy grins on their faces.

"We looooove it!" Becca says. "Can we ride with the top down?"

"Sure," I tell them. "Except I don't know how to put it down."

"No problem," Becca replies.

She saunters over to a group of boys and turns on her smoldering Latina thing. (Becca is such a hottie. She looks like a tall Eva Longoria and could have easily joined Crystal in the elite crowd if she'd wanted.) Within seconds, three boys are hard at work trying to figure out my roof.

Melanie and I share a smile. "You could have gotten them to do that too," I tell her.

Melanie just laughs. "Yeah, if I promised to do their homework for a year."

In no time, the top is down and we're cruising down RBA—Ruby Beach Avenue—listening to the Black Eyed Peas. It's like they're singing just for us and the summer ahead.

> *"Let's get it started ha . . .*
> *Let's get it started in here . . ."*

Becca grabs Melanie's yearbook and starts flipping through it. "You've got to hear what Kevin wrote to our little bookworm." She finds the page and starts to read it. "I hope to see you over the summer - stay sexy."

I can't help but smile at this. Bec and I even sing along with Fergie and the boys to tease Mel a bit.

> *"Let's get it started ha . . .*
> *Let's get it started in here . . ."*

Melanie, of course, blushes. She always blushes. She's had a crush on Kevin

Cavanaugh for years. Even though he's more than a foot taller than she is, they would make the most adorable mismatched couple. That is, they would if it weren't for the one problem that has kept her from acting on that crush.

"He misspelled 'sexy,'" Mel points out. "He wrote s-e-x-i-e."

That's the problem.

Melanie is a total brain. She's our likely valedictorian and is bound for med school. The only way they'll cross paths as adults is if she's on call in the emergency room the night he finally breaks his leg trying to do a backflip on his Jet Ski.

"So, he's no genius," Becca concedes. "Do you want him to proofread your papers?" Her voice drops to a husky whisper. "Or do you want him to make you a woman?"

Melanie laughs and thinks this one over. "Good point. But sexy's a pretty simple word. I think I'd like a guy who could *be* it and *spell* it."

"A reasonable standard," I add in agreement.

Mel smiles at me from the backseat.

"That's why I'm using my insider connections with the mermaid community to hook me up with Mr. Wonderful this summer."

This brings my mood to a crashing halt.

"Hate to break it to you," I say. "But you just lost your inside connection." I tell them all about my meeting with Coach Latham and why I can't swim in the mermaid show.

"Un-freaking-believable!"

Typical Becca. She starts off at outrage and builds from there.

"You should sue," she continues. "We can get one of those shifty-looking lawyers off the back of the phone book."

I explain that it's no use. "I can't jeopardize my chance for a scholarship. I just have to go in and quit."

As I say it, I realize it's true. I really have to go in and quit. This blows.

"This is so ruining our first ride in your car," Melanie adds.

"Why?" I ask, taking an unfair swipe at them. "I thought you'd both be happy. You've been trying to make me miserable ever since I got the job."

"Yeah," Becca says. "But it's all right if *we* make you miserable. *We* love you. It's not okay for some lard butt we don't even know to make you miserable. That's not even close to being okay."

I start to laugh, and so does Melanie. "Lard butt" was the first put-down Becca learned when she came to America. Through the years it has remained a favorite. Every time she says it, I think it's funny.

We're still laughing when I pull the car into the gravel lot at Russell Park. The park stretches for a few blocks and over-looks the beach. It has public restrooms, a picnic area, and a band shell that they use for special events like the Fourth of July. It also has a huge barbecue pit, which is why we come here every year on the last day of school.

Our ritual is simple. We pull out our school planners and write down the name of the one person who has wronged us the most during the year. Then we burn the planners in the barbecue pit and say, "You're fired." Just like Donald Trump, only we thought of it first.

We've been doing this since the eighth grade and as corny as it sounds, it's really fun. We just sit there, kick back, and look forward to summer vacation.

I was going to write Scott Bushnell's name in my planner. He was supposed to take me to the Spring Fling, but he bailed at the last moment to go to a model airplane convention. Although I haven't forgiven him, I'm currently more pissed about the mermaid thing. So, I write down the name of the state athletic association. Their stupid rule has already ruined my summer.

As we watch the planners burn away, Becca tries to lighten the mood. "I have just the thing to cheer you up," she offers.

"What?" I ask skeptically.

"Choice gossip verification."

Mel and I both lean forward in anticipation. Becca is the Queen of Dish. She's had a subscription to *Teen People* since the very first issue. If she says it's good, you can count on it.

"The rumors have gone on long enough," she says dramatically. "So I decided it was time to find out the truth about Crystal's boob job."

She savors the moment and leaves us hanging.

"And . . . ," Mel blurts, almost unable to contain herself.

Bec flashes a huge smile. "They're just as phony as her personality."

"I knew it," Mel gasps.

I'm still skeptical. "How were you able to *confirm* this?"

Becca beams, obviously proud of herself. "At great risk of personal injury, I tripped and fell into her while she was at her locker."

"You tripped?" Mel asks. "On purpose?"

"I slammed right into them," Becca says.

I start to laugh.

"I almost got a black eye from the left one," she adds. "Someday some poor boy's going to get hurt on that thing."

Now I'm laughing so hard, I think I'm going to pee my pants. I can fully picture Becca doing this. After all, she is the one who actually *does* the things that Melanie and I only *talk* about doing.

Becca was the one who got her belly button pierced. (My parents would have killed me.) And she's the one who got a tattoo on her butt. (My parents would have killed themselves.) The tattoo is hilarious. It's a bumble bee, and sometimes when she gets excited, she pokes it with her thumb and goes, "Buzz, buzz, buzz."

"How do they feel?" I ask, unsure if I really want to know.

Bec scrunches her lips while she tries to think of just the right words. "Kind of like those frosting bags you use to ice a birthday cake. But filled *way* too much."

I wish I hadn't asked. I may never look at cake the same way again.

"I'm sorry, but that's disgusting," Mel says, mulling this over. "I can't believe boys really think that's attractive?"

"Surf the Internet," Becca instructs her. "I think you'll find they're okay with it."

It really does amaze me that a girl our age would do something like that to her body. I mean, Crystal was already hot. I just don't get it.

"That's why the Crystals of the world will always have their pick of guys," I say. Then I look down at my own rather unendowed body and add, "And that's why I won't."

"What are you talking about?" Becca asks. "I thought this was going to be the Summer of Love."

"The Summer of Love is fast becoming the Winter of Our Discontent," I say, borrowing a line from AP English. "When I was going to be a mermaid, I thought I could pull it off. But now . . . it's just all wrong."

"What's all wrong?" Mel asks.

"Everything," I say. "My hair. My clothes. My body. Even my name. I mean, *Jane*? When's the last time you heard of someone hot named *Jane*?"

They think for a moment.

"Tarzan and Jane," Becca offers. "She's smoking hot. She's got that whole jungle fever thing going."

"First of all, she's fictional," I say. "Second, she lives with a monkey."

"What about Jane Goodall? She's good-looking *and* smart."

"Who's Jane Goodall?" Becca asks.

"The world's leading primatologist," Mel answers. "You remember that video in biology, with the woman in Africa."

"You know," I tell her. "The English

woman who *also* lives with monkeys."

"Actually, they're chimps," Melanie says. "But that's a little freaky."

"You guys are really not helping here," I tell them. "Face it. I'm Plain Jane. Strictly vanilla."

They're quiet for a moment, and then Melanie speaks up.

"Technically, vanilla is the mother of all ice-cream flavors. Chocolate, Rocky Road, mint chocolate chip—they all start out as vanilla." (She worked at Glenn's Homemade Ice-Cream Shoppe last summer.) "All you've got to do is add the right ingredients."

Becca starts to smile. She's obviously come up with something. As she thinks it over, she absently starts to poke her thumb into her tattoo. "Buzz, buzz, buzz."

"What?" I ask her.

"What if . . . you had a second identity?"

"Ooh," Mel joins in. "Like Peter Parker in *Spider-Man*." (Mel has a total Tobey Maguire fixation.)

"And in addition to being Plain Jane— who we know and love," Bec continues, "you were also . . . Bikini Jane."

"Bikini Jane?" I ask, completely unimpressed.

"Exactly," Becca answers.

"I kind of like it," Mel says. "It's way cheesy. But it gets to the point."

"First of all," I reply, laughing, "I'm missing two very important components of the Bikini Jane outfit. And unless you've got a couple of overfilled frosting bags in your backpack, it's just not going to happen."

Becca shakes her head. "That's not what being Bikini Jane is all about."

"Easy for you to say, Captain Curvaceous."

"No. Bikini Jane is all about attitude. That's what those mermaid girls really have going for them. They project an 'I'm hot' attitude and the boys come running."

"She's right," Melanie says.

The more Becca thinks it over, the more she likes the idea. "This summer, if you meet a boy and you get intimidated—or, if you're in a situation and you're not sure how to act—just ask yourself one thing."

They say it together: "What would Bikini Jane do?"

"That's hot," Becca says. "That'll work."

They keep going at this for a while, acting out different scenarios and offering up what they think Bikini Jane would do in those situations. Each one is funnier than the last, and pretty soon I'm laughing so hard that I'm crying. I've got to hand it to them. I may have no luck when it comes to boys, but when it comes to friends, I've got the best.

Four

This is so not right.

It's the first day of summer vacation and I'm already up at six thirty in the morning. Officially, I've sworn off overpriced coffee until I've paid for the car. But this is an emergency, so I break my Starbucks rule and get a venti cappuccino.

By the time I reach Magic Waters, the caffeine has done its trick and I'm nearly coherent. I need to find my supervisor before orientation starts so I can beg for a different job. (Mermaid show or no mermaid show, I still owe my parents $1,250.)

She's cool about it when I explain my problem, and she even arranges for me to stay in the Entertainment Department. This is great because entertainment pays almost a dollar an hour more than any other department. The job, though, is with the zoo crew. Not great.

The zoo crew is what they call the costumed characters who roam around the park and dance in the parade. A job like that might be cool at a place like Disney World, where the costumes are well made and the characters are beloved. But at Magic Waters, it's like a completely lame school play.

I get assigned to play Eager Beaver.

I'm not joking. That's really his name. Or her name. No one really knows if Eager Beaver is a boy or a girl. They only know that Eager Beaver likes to dance around the Rapid River Log Flume—"The Rootin' Tootinest ride in the Wild Wild West."

Next, I go to the wardrobe warehouse, which could not be freakier. When I open the door I run smack into the disembodied head of Ollie Otter. All the character heads are stored on posts right by the front door. When you're not expecting it, it looks like you've stumbled into some bizarro cartoon headhunter ceremony.

I report to the costume counter, which is manned by a woman who I swear is the actual Mrs. Claus. She's got rosy red cheeks, granny glasses, and a sewing apron.

"Good morning," she says in a manner way too jolly for this time of day. "Who are you?"

"Jane," I answer. "Jane Quincy."

She gives a disapproving look and points her finger at me in a way that makes me want to snap it off.

"You may be Jane Quincy out there"— she motions to the door—"but once you pass through these portals, you become one of our magical characters."

I think this is going to take more than one venti.

"So let's try again. Who are you?"

"Eager Beaver," I mumble, still trying to rub the sleep out of my eyes, hoping this is all a dream.

"Well, you don't sound so eager to me," she says with a laugh. "But we can work on that."

She disappears into a back room and returns with my costume. It's hideous. She hands me a fur body suit that weighs a ton, a pair of four-fingered gloves, and huge black boots that will completely ruin my feet. Then she goes over to the giant rack-o'-heads (God, that freaks me out) and pulls off Eager Beaver's noggin. I don't know why he's so happy, but he's got the biggest buck-toothed smile you ever did see.

I seriously consider running out the door.

Mrs. Claus misreads my dumbfounded state of shock as a case of magical wonder and awe.

She smiles warmly. "Don't worry, dear. You're perfect for Eager Beaver." She says this as though it's a good thing.

"Why is that?" I want to know. But I'm more than a little scared of what the answer might be.

"Because you're so flat-chested," she replies. "The costume won't bind in the bust."

At this point, I want to kill Mrs. Claus. But I'm pretty sure that will cost me my job and ultimately my car. So instead, I just smile. "Lucky me."

"Why don't you go try it on," she adds.

The costume, me, and my flat chest all head into the locker room, which reeks of polyester, sweat, and Fiberglas. Despite the assurances of Mrs. Claus, the costume could not be more uncomfortable.

The fur body (think bad shag carpet) is about eight million degrees. Right from the start it makes my skin itch. The Fiberglas head has only two teensy eye slits, which makes it impossible to see. The head also weighs so much that if I lean just a little too much one way or another, I lose my balance.

The worst part, though, is the tail. Eager Beaver's got a gigantic tail. It's even gigantic by cartoon standards. It pulls down on my butt so much, I feel like my pants are falling down.

I spend the next few minutes walking around the locker room trying to develop my "beaver legs." In just a few minutes, I manage to trip over my tail, knock down a potted plant, trip over my tail again, smack into a Coke machine, and slam headfirst into the wall of lockers. (Altogether, not unlike the night Becca and I mixed rum and Diet Coke under the mistaken belief that they were to be blended in equal amounts.)

Orientation turns out to be a lot like the first day of school. By the time I figure out where the bathroom is, everyone else has already broken up into little groups. It doesn't take long to see that there's a pecking order at Magic Waters, just like there is at Ruby Beach High.

The mermaids sit alone at the top of the food chain. They're the stars. (They even wear matching baby blue warm-ups with their names stitched just above their oh-so-perfect left breasts.) The zoo crew is somewhere in the middle just above food service and the janitorial staff.

After an initial welcome speech, everyone goes off into smaller groups with their departments.

While Crystal and the mer-chicks pose for their lobby photos, I learn the beaver dance from a "choreographer" whose name is pronounced "Chris" but spelled "Krys." The dance is pretty much just me hopping around and shaking my tail. Krys, of course, is not satisfied.

"You're a beaver, not a bunny," he says, clapping his hands to the beat.

I have no idea what he means, but I act like I do and I just keep hopping and shaking. Luckily I am rescued by Platypus Rex, who informs Krys that Ollie Otter is having big trouble mastering the parade march.

When Krys rushes over to help Ollie, Rex hustles me out a side door to a patio.

"You looked like you needed a break," he says as he takes off his platypus head and plops down on a bench.

"Thank you," I tell him as I ditch my giant beaver head. "My name's Jane."

"Grayson." We sort of shake hands, which is not easy in our bulky costumes.

I try to get a good image of him, but it's hard. His hair is all stuffed into a bandanna and his face is flushed from wearing the costume. I'm sure I'm not looking my best right now either.

It turns out that Grayson's a senior at Fletcher—our rival high school. He is in his third summer as Platypus Rex. Unlike Krys and Mrs. Claus, he doesn't seem to take it so seriously.

He tells me the various zoo crew rules, which are plentiful. Characters are not allowed to talk (because it breaks the magic), and you can only sign autographs after special training to make sure you do it right. (I'm not kidding.)

You're never allowed to take off your head when you're in a guest area because it really freaks kids out. (After my first encounter with the rack-o'-heads, I can relate.)

He also warns me that every single kid who comes into the park will feel the need to pull my tail. Despite my natural instinct, it is not all right for me to slug them when they do this.

We chat some more until Krys finds us and orders us back inside for more practice. Two hours later, I stumble back into the locker room and collapse on the bench. I am totally exhausted. My face and hair are so covered in sweat that I don't even know where to begin.

As if on cue, Crystal and the other mermaids come in from their photo shoot. They don't mock or pick or even notice my existence. They don't have to.

They just smile their perfect smiles, toss their perfect hair, and heave their perfect (and fake) breasts. I was supposed to be one of them. I was supposed to be in a bikini, working on my tan and flirting with boys. Instead, I'm a giant beaver in a fur suit getting my tail yanked by bratty kids.

I watch them sashay by and realize a horrifying truth: The conspiracy to ruin my life is now complete.

Five

After a week at Tragic Waters, I feel like I'm a walking bruise. Every inch of my body aches, and there's a constant throbbing in my shoulders courtesy of the giganto Fiberglas head. As if that's not bad enough, last night I had my first Eager Beaver nightmare. (Grayson warned me that everyone has them.)

In the dream, I'm back in school but no one can hear me. I scream, shout, yell, everything, but the only response I get is people pointing and laughing. I run into the girls' room, look in the mirror, and see that I'm in my beaver costume. Then Mrs. Claus comes out of one of the stalls, raps me on the paw, and says, "No talking in costume!"

If this keeps up, I'll need a psychiatrist by Labor Day.

Today's my first day of swim lessons, so I'm going to hit the pool early and start on Coach Latham's workout routine.

I stumble into the kitchen and pour myself a bowl of Honeycombs. I'm so out of it, I don't even notice my dad sitting at the table eating his breakfast.

"Look who's up," he says, all bright and cheery. "Aren't you a busy little beaver?"

My dad lives to tell bad jokes. He considers it his gift to the world. I realize that I have to nip this in the bud or it will go on all summer long.

I wave my cereal spoon at him with as much menace as I can manage. "That's not funny, Dad."

"What? You don't like the little beaver wordplay?"

"No, I don't."

"Kind of *gnaws* at you, doesn't it?"

"Stop it, Dad."

"Maybe you should *lodge* a complaint."

That one almost gets me. I'm trying

not to laugh on principle, but he doesn't make it easy. He's a really funny guy. I overcome the urge and give him my toughest look. "That's enough."

"So you're not going to laugh?" he asks.

"No, I'm not."

"Dam!" he says.

"Beaver, dam. I get it, Dad. Still not funny." As I say this, I finally break and start to laugh. Some of my milk shoots up my nose, which is just what he wanted.

"Now I can go to work," he says as he finishes his last piece of toast. He gets up, leans over, and gives me a kiss on the forehead. "I love you, Janey."

"Love you, too, Daddy," I tell him. "Stay safe."

I always say this when he goes to work. He's a captain with the Ruby Beach Fire Department, and even though I know he's careful, a part of me worries every time he leaves the house.

On my way to the Y, I break my Starbucks rule again and get another venti cappuccino. (I admit it. I'm an addict.) I get to the pool an hour before my lesson so I can put in some training laps. USC's about three thousand miles away, and it seems like Coach Latham wants to see if I could swim the whole way.

The water feels great, and the exercise helps work the soreness out of my shoulders. When I'm done, I feel like a new woman. I look around at all the kids arriving for lessons. They don't look so bad. I can handle any of them as long as there isn't a barfer. (Barfers are the worst. You've got to evacuate the whole pool and clean it up. No money is worth that.)

I see the director of aquatics heading my way. She's smiling and rapping her clipboard with a pencil, which means she needs a favor. I brace myself.

"Would you mind doing a home lesson instead?" she asks.

Home lessons are never a good sign. Since they cost triple the normal rate, the only parents willing to pay for them are the rich, bitchy types who can't be bothered to drive their kids to the Y and wait around for an hour.

"Seriously?" I ask, trying to decide if I want to be bothered with this or try to push it off onto somebody else.

"The kid's name is Alex Walker, and apparently he is a total klutz around the water," she says. "The mother specifically asked for our top instructor."

This may just be buttering me up, but I'm okay with that. She hands me a registration form, and my worst fears are confirmed when I see the address. The house is on Lake Shelby, which means it's a total mansion. No doubt they'll make me feel like a servant just for showing up. Still, I remind myself that the triple rate will help put a dent in the money I owe my parents for the car.

"I'll do it," I tell her. "But you owe me."

I throw on a pair of gym shorts and a Ruby Beach Bobcats T-shirt over my bathing suit and head for my car. Whoever owned the Cabrio before me put in a great sound system, so I turn some Gwen Stefani up full blast as I drive over to Lake Shelby.

Gwen always puts me in a good mood.

As expected, the house is a totally impressive showpiece. But as I make my way down the incredibly long driveway, I see some eye candy even more impressive than the house. He's about my age and he's pushing a lawn mower.

Like all of the other homes on Lake Shelby, the Walker estate has lush and beautiful landscaping. But, unlike the others, theirs comes with a lawn boy who's pretty lush himself.

He's tall (I love tall) and has a great tan. He's got deep brown eyes that I could totally get lost in. His hair is a mess, but still cute in a surf boy kind of way. When he sees me, he stops his mower and flashes a smile that should be illegal.

All of a sudden, I hear the voices of Bec and Mel in my head, and they're both saying the same thing:

What would Bikini Jane do?

Flirt, I answer silently.

I smile back and sneak a quick peek in my rearview mirror. Not good. It's my moment of need, and my hair is doing absolutely nothing for me. I didn't put anything in it because my big plans for the day were to jump in a pool and put on a beaver costume.

Be confident.

What am I worried about? He's doing

44

lawn work. His hair's a total mess too.

Relax.

Flirting does not come naturally to me, but since he stopped his mower, the least I can do is get out and go say hello. After all, we're both just hardworking teens summoned to the mansion to earn a little cash.

"Hello," I say as I slowly run my fingers through my hair, trying to mask its total lack of body. Becca taught me this, but I can't really do it like she does.

"Hi," he answers back. "May I help you?"

Hot and polite—nice combo. I try to act cool, which is hard because I'm about to hyperventilate. "I'm here to see Mrs. Walker."

"Sorry," he says. "She just left."

That's strange. She should be here for the lesson.

"What about Mr. Walker?" I ask, trying not to stare too deep into those eyes.

"He left too. They were together."

"They're both gone?" I ask, suddenly getting pissed.

"Yep," he says. "It's just me."

I forget about dreamy lawn boy for a minute and think about bratty swim lesson boy.

"I don't believe it," I say.

"Is there a problem?"

I can't help myself. I start to vent. "You bet there is. I just drove all the way out here to give swim lessons to their son, who is apparently so uncoordinated that he can't be seen in public. And they don't even have the common decency to be here."

With no warning I've gone straight to Insane Jane. I try to put on the brakes, but it's too late. (And I wonder why I never have a boyfriend.)

"Wow!" he says, obviously surprised by my outburst.

I can't believe I vented all over him, I'm so not playing this right. I try to change course. "I'm sorry. I shouldn't bother you with my problems. It's just . . ."

"That's okay," he says. "I understand."

He stares at me for a moment, and I have to admit it kind of freaks me out. This is beyond embarrassing, and my instinct is to end the conversation and bolt. But he's cracking a crooked little smile that makes me think we've got a chance for some kind of memorable first contact.

What would Bikini Jane do?

I chance it.

"I'm Jane, by the way," I say, offering my hand.

"Like the Maroon 5 CD," he answers with a firm and altogether sexy handshake. *Songs About Jane.* (Hello, why didn't my friends come up with this when I was having my name crisis?)

Play it cool.

"I hate that CD," I tell him.

"You do?"

"It's bad enough I had to dump the guy. But then, to keep hearing about it on the radio. I wish he'd just let it go."

This brings a laugh. "So, you're *the* Jane?"

"Absolutely. Don't you recognize me?"

I use my hands to fan out my hair like the girl on the CD cover, and he laughs some more. Maybe Bec and Mel were right about Bikini Jane. I don't know who this girl is, but he seems to like her.

"Well, it's nice to meet someone so . . . inspirational. My name is Alex."

Okay. I'm slow. I admit it. That's why I still don't see the problem. (That and the fact that I'm pretending to be this confident girl who just randomly talks to hot guys.)

"That's funny," I say. "Their son's name is Alex too."

"I know." There's not even a hint of anger in his voice. But finally, I see the problem.

"Oh, my God," I answer as I look into the dreamy eyes. "Oh, my God. You're not the lawn boy."

"No," he says in a way that kind of sounds like he's enjoying this. "I'm the uncoordinated son who can't be seen in public."

To borrow a phrase from Becca:

Un-freaking-believable.

Six

I spend the next five minutes apologizing over and over again. Each time, he says it's okay, and each time I can't believe what I've done.

"It's just, when I saw you cutting the grass," I try to explain.

"You figured that no one who lived in a house like this would actually mow their own lawn?"

I nod. "I guess so."

"Well, you're right," he says. "I don't live here. At least not usually. I'm just spending the summer with my dad. He thinks stuff like this builds character."

"Still," I answer, "it was wrong of me. Is

there any way I can make it up to you?"

"You could stop apologizing."

"You're right. I'm sorry. I mean, anything else? Just name it."

"You can keep all of this on the down low," he answers.

"What, me making a fool of myself?" I say. "I hadn't planned on telling anyone."

"No, I mean, me learning how to swim," he says.

"Why do you want that to be a secret?" I ask.

"What do you call the first level of swim lessons?"

"Pollywogs," I answer.

"That's why. It's bad enough that I'm seventeen years old and trying to earn my Pollywog badge. But—for this summer, at least—I live in a house on a big lake and we've got a huge pool and I am completely and totally afraid of the water."

I laugh. I try not to, but I can't help myself.

"This isn't going to work."

"No, it'll work," I tell him. "I won't laugh. And I won't tell anybody."

He looks at me, and I melt.

"Okay," he says. "Then you are completely forgiven."

"And your secret is safe. Show me the pool."

We walk around to the back of the house and I see that "huge" was an understatement. The pool is one of those giant, landscaped deals with a rocky waterfall on one side and a hot tub on the other.

Alex is flat terrified to be near it. It's funny, because he's big and strong and yet so vulnerable at the same time. (And I thought Starbucks was addictive.)

"Where do you want to start?" I ask him.

"As far from the water as possible," he says with a smile. "Like maybe the front yard."

I've dealt with lots of kids who were scared of the water. And the trick was to get them to relax.

"How about this?" I offer. "Let's sit next to the hot tub and we can just dangle our legs in. It's only a couple of feet deep."

He eyes it suspiciously. "I guess that would be okay."

I lead him over there, and we sit down.

Without realizing it, he grabs hold of my leg and it kind of sends an electric charge through my body. (It's like the classic horror movie date. Except I'm the big strong one, he's the scared one, and the pool is the homicidal maniac running around with a chainsaw.)

Becca says that boys love to talk about themselves, and I figure she should know. So, I get him started and he goes from there. He tells me that he lives in Washington, D.C., with his mother. He's spending the summer here while she's on the road making a documentary.

"Like on the History Channel?" I ask.

"Exactly," he says, clearly pleased with my reaction. "You watch that stuff?"

"All the time," I say. (I leave out the part about being forced to watch against my will.) "I love documentaries. They're like *The Real World*, only real."

He laughs, and I silently thank my father. We continue talking, and he relaxes more and more. Luckily for me, he's still tense enough that he keeps his hand on my leg.

Finally, I ask him the big question.

"Why are you so scared of the water?"

He thinks about it for a moment. "When I was seven years old, my family went on vacation and there was a pool at the hotel. I was so excited that I rushed ahead of my parents and jumped in. But when I went underwater, my foot broke through the drain cover and got stuck.

"I couldn't get to the surface and I started to panic. I tried to call for my mom, but I couldn't make any sounds. I just kept swallowing water until I passed out. My mom dived in and rescued me. She did CPR right by the pool."

"Wow! You've got some mom."

"It's weird," he continues. "Even though she's the one who saved me, she's always felt guilty about it. So she's spent the past ten years keeping me as far away from water as possible. My dad, on the other hand, thinks I should tackle my fear head-on."

"More character building," I say.

"Exactly. And since I'm with him for the summer, I'm going to learn how to swim."

It's an amazing story, and when he's

done, I look down and see that he is now holding my hand. There's nothing flirty about it. But it feels great.

"So can you help me?" he asks. "Can you teach me how to swim?"

"Absolutely," I say. (I'm also more than willing to sit next to the pool and hold your hand for as long as you'd like.)

"What's the trick to teaching someone who's scared of the water?" he asks.

"Whenever I've done it in the past," I tell him, "I stand in the middle of the pool with a favorite toy."

He thinks about this for a moment.

"I don't think that would work for me," he says. "If you took my iPod into the pool, it would probably get ruined."

I laugh and say, "Then I guess I'll have to find something else that will entice you into the water."

He looks at me for a moment.

"I think you'll do pretty good all by yourself," he says.

OH, MY GOD! OH, MY GOD! OH, MY GOD!

Is that a line? I don't know. No one's ever given me a line before.

I try to think of something witty or sexy or at least verbal to say in response. But when I open my mouth, all that comes out is some sort of sound like a bike tire going flat.

Still, he's smiling and I'm along for the ride. After what seems like an eternity, I tell him that our hour's up and I have to head to my other job.

In reality, I have to jump into my car, scream my lungs out, hyperventilate, and call Becca and Mel to fill them in on all the details. The problem is, they'll want to know what he looks like and I won't be able to do him justice.

An idea.

"First, though," I say lamely, holding up my camera phone, "I need to take a picture."

"Why?"

It's a reasonable question. I have no reasonable answer. I think for a moment.

"For your certificate. When you pass your swim test, you get a Pollywog certificate with your picture on it."

I don't know if he buys it or not, but he nods like he does. "Just let me put on my shirt," he says.

"No," I blurt a little too loudly for comfort. Then I try to cover. "I mean, don't bother, it won't even show up in the picture. It's just a head shot."

Total lie. I take a full-body picture and instantly e-mail it to Becca and Mel.

Big mistake.

We walk around the front to my car and before I can even get there, my phone starts ringing. I look at the caller ID. It's Becca.

"Who is Mr. Hottie?" she yells. I hope he can't hear her.

"Don't worry, Mom," I answer. "I'll pick up the marmalade on the way home."

"Marmalade" is our panic word. It's a word everybody knows, but that you never really use.

"No way," she answers back much softer. "Is he right there?"

"Yes," I say, acting as though I were still talking to my mom.

"Is he still shirtless?" she asks.

I hang up.

Luckily, we've reached the car.

"So, same time tomorrow?" Now I'm just trying to make it out alive.

"Perfect," he says.

I hurry into the car and start to pull away. I wave good-bye and take one last glorious eyeful. He waves back and flashes a smile so lethal that I almost back over his mailbox. Still, I'm able to keep my calm until I reach the street and start to hyperventilate.

I speed-dial Becca.

"Who is he?!"

I can tell by the sound in the background that she's riding her exercise bike.

"Just a boy," I say, playing it cool.

"Right," Becca pants as she pedals away. "And Tom Welling is just a little bit cute."

Before I can respond, the phone rings again.

"That's Mel," I say. "I'll put her on three-way."

Mel doesn't even wait for me to say hello. "Who? What? When? Where?" she asks rapid-fire.

Judging by their reaction, my first impressions were right on target. Alex *is* completely gorgeous.

"I'll tell you everything tonight at my place," I promise them. "But I'm going to need some help."

"What kind of help?" Becca asks.

I can't believe I'm about to say this. "Extreme Makeover: Bikini Jane Edition."

I can't see them, but I know they're smiling.

Seven

I'm sitting in a chair in the middle of my bedroom and I'm no longer a person. I'm an object. Becca and Melanie circle around me, poking and prodding like I'm a car they're thinking of buying.

Becca gives me a long, hard look. "When you say 'makeover,' what exactly are you talking about? Something out of *CosmoGirl*, like learn how to do Lindsay Lohan's eye shadow?"

I shake my head. "No, I want something out of the Witness Relocation Program—so my own family won't even recognize me. We need to take the Bikini Jane concept and turn it into reality before Alex's swim lesson tomorrow morning."

Melanie smiles. "Now we're talking."

They've been waiting for this for a long time. It's not like I don't care about my appearance. I really do. It's just that my style is pretty limited. I usually go for jeans and T-shirts. Hair and makeup are a problem because I spend about half my life in a swimming pool. I'm just happy when I don't smell like chlorine. But now I'm ready to go for broke.

It may take a village to raise a child, but I'm counting on two best friends, half the Clinique counter, and the complete first season of *Alias* on DVD to unleash my inner Aniston.

Before we get started, Becca makes an announcement. "I want to remind you of one key thing." She reaches into her backpack and pulls out the picture of Alex in all his shirtless glory. She tapes it to my mirror. "You've got to keep your eyes on the prize."

I nod in agreement. "Eyes on the prize. I'm ready."

What follows is a lot like orientation at Magic Waters. Except, instead of Krys teaching me the Beaver dance, Becca's showing me the Sydney Strut—named in honor of Jennifer Garner's character and the kick ass, sexy way she walks. (With the DVD, we can break it down frame-by-frame, which really helps.)

Becca demonstrates it with breath-taking ease. When she moves she's all curves and inertia, with no regard for Newton's Laws of Motion. (If she weren't my best friend, I'd really hate her.)

I try it, and the effect is very different: mostly elbows and kneecaps flying out in odd directions.

Becca's undeterred. "Heel, toe, heel, toe," she coaches. "Overlap your feet and swivel your hips."

I try again and it's still not there.

"We want an *Alias* walk," she says. "Not an alien walk."

This is going to take all night.

While I keep practicing, Melanie goes to work on my wardrobe. She digs around my swimsuit drawer but can't find anything that pleases her. They're all racing suits. They were designed to reduce drag and repel water, not to enhance cleavage and attract boys.

"None of these will work," she proclaims. "We may need a bikini."

I stop mid-Sydney. "No way."

"I'm just saying . . ."

Becca joins in. "Mel's right. You can't be *Bikini* Jane without a bikini. That would make you . . . One-Piece Jane."

I glare at Melanie. I glare at Becca. They know I can be self-conscious about my body. "You said the bikini thing was about attitude, not about actually wearing one. You gave a speech and everything."

"I know," Becca answers. "I was lying."

"It would be ridiculous," I say. "No one gives a lesson in one. Don't you think he'd notice?"

"That's the point," says Melanie. "For him to *notice*."

"Besides," Becca adds, "there's not a seventeen-year-old boy on this planet who doesn't want his swim instructor to wear one. It's like something out of an Aerosmith video."

After some more debate, I'm finally willing to concede their point. But that doesn't change the fact that I don't actually own a bikini.

"No," Becca says. "But your sister does."

That's an understatement. Kendra is what we affectionately call a "summer slut." Her entire June-July-August wardrobe is designed to showcase her killer abs. (She does so many sit-ups, her sorority sisters call her "Captain Crunch.")

She's been home from college for three weeks, which means she and Erik have already had their third annual Memorial Day "I missed you so much, can't we get back together?" talk. (This will undoubtedly lead to their third annual Labor Day "I never want to see your stupid face again" fight.) But for now, she's out of the house and her clothes are completely unprotected.

Since Kendra was the one who inspired all of this madness with her "Make this summer count" advice, I'm able to rationalize the petty theft. In all, we "borrow" three bikinis, some short-shorts with ALPHA CHI OMEGA written across the butt, and a cool pair of Ray-Bans.

It's funny, because the moment I put on Kendra's clothes, the walk comes more naturally. Pretty soon I'm Sydney strutting all over the place.

"That's hot," Mel says with a nod of approval.

"Scorching," adds Becca.

Suddenly, I'm having fun.

"What next?" I ask.

Becca reaches over and feels my hair. "We've got to scrunch this. Give it that Teri Hatcher look."

Doing anything to my hair is ridiculous when you consider that the moment I dive in the pool, it won't matter anymore. But it will take us three to four minutes to walk from the front door to the pool, and I'm taking advantage of every second I can get.

I've never scrunched my hair before, but the girls help me and it's pretty easy. All I do is wash and towel-dry it. Then I comb it out with my fingers and scrunch a little product into it. (No brushes allowed!) After that, we put it up in what Bec calls "a big freakin' bun" and let it sit. While it's piled on top of my head, we move on to makeup.

Usually pools and cosmetics don't mix. Luckily for me, Melanie is a master of minimal makeup for maximum effect. She flips through a magazine until she finds a great picture of Sophia Bush. (Personally, I don't get the whole *One Tree Hill* thing, but she is gorgeous.)

With the picture as our guide, Melanie goes to work with a Bad Gal eye pencil and then hands me a small pot of fuchsia lip gloss. We experiment with some different nail polish until we find a perfect shade of pink from MAC.

"That's it," Melanie says, backing away so as not to disturb a thing. "We're done."

I let my hair down and look at myself in the mirror. I know it's me. But it sure doesn't look like me.

"You look great," Becca says.

I'm not convinced. "You think?"

"I don't think, I *know*. Still, we need a dress rehearsal."

"A what?"

Becca grabs a FOND OF BEING BLONDE tee. "Put this on," she says. "We're going to Mama Taco's."

Mama Taco's is our hangout. It's an old wooden shack right on the beach. It serves the best Tex-Mex in the state and it's always packed. Becca lays out her plan as we drive over.

"Mel and I are going to go in first," she instructs. "Give us a few minutes to get a table. Then you come in and do your Sydney strut straight to the counter. Place an order and then come sit down with us."

"How is this a dress rehearsal for a swim lesson?" I ask.

"We kind of figure you've got the swimming thing down, Aquagirl," Becca says. "This is about guys. We'll be watching them, and hopefully they'll be watching you. By the time you sit down, we'll know exactly how good a job we've done."

I feel like a total doofus as I wait in the parking lot. It's bad enough that I'm doing this. But it will be ten times worse when I do it and none of the guys notice me.

I wait a few minutes and then I go in. It is beyond awkward as I try to do the walk and look confident without tripping over myself. I order a Coke and some chicken nachos. I can't imagine that any guy has so much as looked my way. But as I walk to the table, I'm amazed by what I see.

Becca and Melanie are grinning from ear to ear.

Eight

I wake up with a bad case of makeover hangover. It's like a normal hangover, except that the empty bottles scattered around the room used to hold nail polish. As I get dressed, my mind is a throbbing blur of hairdos and fashion don'ts.

I stop and look at myself in the mirror. A nice boy has asked me for help. Okay, a *smoking hot* nice boy. And how did I meet the challenge? I stole my sister's clothes and learned to walk like a supermodel/government assassin.

I'm pathetic.

But, damn, my hair looks *great*.

The supermodel-assassin moves come

in handy for my escape from the house. There may not be any foreign agents to elude, but running into family members could be just as dangerous. My parents' curiosity about hair and makeup for a swim lesson would be bad enough. Kendra seeing me wearing her clothes could prove fatal.

Within seconds, I'm in the Cabrio and on the road. Everything is going perfectly.

Then the music starts.

I'm a firm believer in Radio Karma: When you start the car, the first song you hear is a message from the music gods about the day ahead.

Radio Karma kick-started the summer as we drove away from school with the Black Eyed Peas singing "Let's Get It Started." And now Radio Karma is kicking my butt as I drive toward Alex's house with some bad alt-rock group screaming away. I don't recognize the group or the song, but some of the lyrics stand out.

> *"She's got problems . . .*
> *She had to suffer some"*

I reach down to change the station, but it's too late. The music gods have spoken, and this is the song they have given me. What kind of message are they sending? I try to twist it into something positive, but it's useless.

"She's got problems.
And more problems to come."

Whatever he's screeching about now has got to be bad.

The song is just terrible, and there's nothing I can do about it. By the time it ends, I'm mental. Maybe this whole Bikini Jane thing is a mistake. I don't want problems and I don't want to suffer. Then the DJ says the name of the group:

Jane's Addiction.

Slowly a smile starts to form.

What if the music gods weren't giving me a song? What if they were giving me a group? I work it out like a geometry proof.

I'm Jane.

I'm addicted to dreamy guys with great personalities.

Alex is a dreamy guy with a great personality.

Therefore, Alex is Jane's Addiction.

Radio Karma. Where would I be without it?

When I pull up to the house, there's no sign of Alex doing more yard work. This gives me a moment to collect my thoughts before I knock on the door. All of this is virgin territory for me. (Okay, technically, everything is virgin territory for me.) I've been Bikini Jane for less than twenty-four hours and I'm already exhausted. I hope it'll get easier.

That's when I hear a voice behind me.

"Are you going to knock or are you just going to stand there?"

It's Alex. He must have walked around from the side of the house. I'm sure I look like a total idiot just staring at the door. But the key to my new persona is confidence, so I fake it.

"That depends," I tell him. "When we get to the pool, are you going to jump in or are you just going to dangle your feet in the water?"

He laughs, and so do I.

"I'll lead you into the house," he says. "And you can lead me into the pool."

"Sounds good."

The inside of the house is even more impressive than the outside. Everything about it is big and expensive, but also tasteful.

"This is a beautiful home," I say.

"It's not a home, it's a trophy," he answers. "My dad won some big lawsuit and suddenly he became Mr. Mansion. The house my mom and I live in is more my style. It's about the size of the living room."

I'm sure he's offering some great insight into his personality, but I'm too busy trying to keep the walk going. In my head, I can hear Becca coaching me.

Overlap your feet. Swivel your hips.

As we reach the kitchen, something catches his eye. "You seem different today," he says, giving me a quick once-over.

How about my hair, my face, my clothes, the way I walk, or the slight emphasis on my Southern accent to make me seem more feminine?

"Nope," I say. "It's the same me as

yesterday, except this time I'm not ranting like a madwoman."

He looks again and smiles. "That must be it."

Becca says you can always count on guys not to notice things. She knows what she's talking about.

We're fine until we reach the pool, and he instantly tenses up. I realize that he truly has a problem and that I can help him with it. I try to give him a little pep talk.

"I'm not the type to brag, but I am an excellent swimmer. I'm even a state champion. I promise that I won't let anything happen to you around the water. You've got to trust me and relax."

"You're a state champion?" he says, impressed. "Really?"

"Really," I reply. I wasn't fishing for a compliment with that one, but I'm glad he noticed.

Still, he's not satisfied. "Do you know CPR?"

"Are you kidding? My dad is a captain with the fire department. I've been a certified instructor since I was twelve."

He relaxes a bit, which is more than I

can say for myself. Despite what Becca and Melanie said, I still feel like a total idiot giving a swim lesson in a bikini. I've just got to do it like taking off a Band-Aid—in one swift motion.

I pull off my shirt, toss it to the ground, and drop my shorts. After a long beat, I finally look up at him. He doesn't say a thing, but I swear I hear him make a sound like a bicycle tire going flat.

Nice to meet you, Bikini Jane.

"Are you ready?"

He nods. "I think so."

I jump in the water. (Good-bye, scrunchy hair. You were nice while you lasted.)

"Jump in!" I tell him.

Instead of actually jumping in, he sits down on the edge of the pool and carefully lowers himself into the shallow end. He's trying to be brave, which is extremely cute.

"I'll make you a deal," I tell him as he clutches on to the side for dear life. "For every five minutes you give me in the water, we can break for five and sit by the pool and talk."

"Deal," he says.

We go to shake on it, but he's holding on to the side so tightly that I end up shaking his elbow.

"The first thing you have to do is put your head underwater," I tell him.

"Shouldn't we build to that?" he asks.

This is the difference between teaching a kid and teaching someone older. When you tell seven-year-olds to do something, they just do it. When you tell seventeen-year-olds, they want reasons.

"It's the thing you're most scared of and it's the thing you have to do in order to swim," I explain.

"I can practice putting my *arm* underwater like this?" He smiles as he dips his shoulder under the surface. He's joking, kind of.

"How tall are you, Alex?"

"Six one."

Wow. Just the sound of that is sexy.

"How deep is the water right here?"

He looks over at the side of the pool and frowns. "Three feet."

I let the math sink in for a moment. "All I'm asking is two seconds underwater.

If there's any problem, all you've got to do is stand up."

He gives me an uncertain look, and I do my best to be reassuring.

"Trust me."

For some reason, that calms him. He smiles and nods. "I do trust you." Then he bends over so that just his face goes under. It isn't pretty and it isn't graceful, but it's a step in the right direction.

Over the next hour, he gets more and more comfortable going under the water. (And I get more and more comfortable wearing a bikini while talking to a hot guy.) Every five minutes, I give him a break and we get out of the pool and talk. We cover everything from school to music to what colleges we're considering. His favorites are American history, classic rock, and the University of Virginia.

He also mentions that he's gotten a job at the tennis shop in the Lake Shelby Country Club. It's more of his father's character-building plan.

"Maybe I can give you tennis lessons," he says. "After you've taught me how to swim."

"I don't think so," I tell him.

"Why not?"

I laugh as I make up a childhood trauma to match his. "You see, when I was seven, I was on vacation with my family and I got stuck in a tennis net. I tried and tried, but I couldn't get out until my dad pulled me free. It was terrible, and now I'm frightened of tennis."

"I've heard of that," he says with a laugh. "I think it's called Sharapova-phobia. I can help you. I just have to come up with something that will inspire you to go onto the court again."

I think about it for a moment and decide to go for broke.

"I think you'd do pretty good all by yourself," I say.

We look into each other's eyes for a moment. Like I said, he's got deep, dreamy eyes.

"That's the stupidest line I've ever heard," he says. Then he pushes me into the water.

As I fall, I instinctively grab his arm and pull him in with me. (Not a good idea.) We hit with a big splash, and he starts to flail around.

It's a frantic couple of moments before he remembers to stand up. Even though we're toward the deep end, he's tall enough to stand on his tiptoes and keep his head out of the water.

"Was that a test?" he asks, trying to cover his nervousness with a joke.

"No, that was an accident," I tell him. "Are you okay?"

"Yes," he says. "It was my fault. I shouldn't have pushed you."

I see the clock on the wall and realize that we're running late. I've got to hurry over to Magic Waters.

"Let's get you out of the pool," I tell him. "I've got to go."

We climb out and towel off. He's quiet for a minute as he gets over the adrenaline rush of falling into the pool.

"So, where do you go from here?" he asks. "Another lesson?"

"No, I'm off to Tragic Waters."

"What's Tragic Waters?"

"That's what most people around here call Magic Waters."

"The place with the mermaids?"

"That's the one," I tell him.

"I've seen the billboard. And I can't imagine a worse idea for a theme park. It's all about water."

"Pretty much."

"Well, you'll never catch me there," he says with a laugh. "What do you do? Are you one of the mermaids?"

I go to answer, but my brain just freezes up. Bikini Jane is real. But there's no way that Bikini Jane is also a giant beaver. I just can't tell him. And then, it comes out. I can't believe it, but I also can't stop it.

"You guessed it. I'm a mermaid."

Nine

"I am the scum you scrape out of the shower."

"That's a bit dramatic, don't you think?" Melanie says as she pulls the bag of popcorn out of the microwave.

"No, it's a fitting description," I reply. "For years I've accused Crystal of being a two-faced liar. And now, the first time I'm alone with a boy, I do the same thing. I lie right to his face. I'm no better than she is."

Mel brings the popcorn over to the couch and plops it down between us. "I think you're making way too much of this. After all, you were *almost* a mermaid. So you *almost* told the truth."

It's Wednesday, which means Becca has family night and Mel and I have junk food on the couch night. We usually watch *Smallville* for our weekly Tom Welling fix and *American Idol* for our weekly "Oh, thank God there's someone more pathetic than me" fix.

Right now, Simon is attacking some poor girl who has screeched her way through "Milkshake." He calls her a worthless piece of garbage, and I can't help but think he's describing me. (Mel was right: I am way dramatic.)

I'm in such a funk that I don't even laugh when he says he may never be able to drink a milkshake again.

Melanie looks over at me. "Would you just get over yourself? You were in a bad mood all through *Smallville*, and it was an episode where he took off his shirt three times. Now you're going to be in a bad mood all through *Idol*?"

"I just can't believe I did something so stupid," I say.

"Welcome to Girl Land. We all do stupid things because of guys. It's normal behavior."

"Really?"

"Definitely," she says.

I think about this for a moment and turn to her. "Then tell me something stupid you've done because of a guy."

"No way," she shoots back. "I'm trying to watch *Idol*."

"If you do, then I'll know it's true," I answer. "But if you don't, then I'll think it's because you haven't ever done something stupid because of a guy."

She rolls her eyes. "This is what you want? Me to humiliate myself for your entertainment?"

"It's not what I want. It's what I need."

She takes a slow sip of her Diet Dr Pepper. "Okay. But you have to promise not to tell anybody—including Becca."

Uh-oh, this must be good. I try not to look too excited, so I lean back in the couch.

"I promise."

She closes her eyes, and I can tell she's still debating whether to tell me.

"Do you remember the field trip that the Spanish Club took to Disney World in the seventh grade?"

Seventh grade?

"Vaguely," I say.

"Well, that was the year I first had a crush on Kevin Cavanaugh."

I can't help but comment. "You mean the same Kevin Cavanaugh you still have a crush on, even though he can't spell 'sexy'?"

"That's the one. Well, I kind of stalked him on the field trip and we ended up riding the Pirates of the Caribbean together. About halfway through, something happened and the ride stopped for a few minutes. So we were just stuck there, with nothing to do. We certainly didn't have anything to talk about. So we started kissing."

I can't believe it. I have never heard any of this before. "You slut! How could you not tell me that you made out with Kevin Cavanaugh on the Pirates of the Caribbean?"

"We didn't make out," she answers. "We just kissed a little. Nothing too big . . . but it was my first kiss. Anyway, on the bus ride home, he gave me a Mickey Mouse lollipop. I don't know why, but he did."

"Maybe he thought you had bad breath," I add.

She gives me a look. "Do you want me to tell the story or not?"

"Sorry. I'll be quiet."

"Because it was a Spanish Club trip he called it *el lollipop del amor*—'the lollipop of love.' He thought that was really smooth."

Now I start to laugh hysterically. In fact, I laugh so hard that it takes a few moments for me to catch my breath. "That's good and all, but I asked you to tell me something stupid that you did for a guy—not something stupid that a guy did for you."

"I'm not done," she says curtly.

Suddenly, I realize where she's going. "Oh, my God! You still have the lollipop!"

She takes another hit of Diet Dr Pepper. "It's in the bottom drawer of my jewelry box."

I rush into her room. There, underneath a pearl necklace and a pair of hoop earrings, I find an old, cracked, pathetic, and completely adorable Mickey Mouse lollipop. I bring it back into the family room and dangle it in front of her.

"I can't believe you've saved this since the seventh grade."

She snaps it out of my hand and carefully sets it on the table. "Like I said, we all do stupid and irrational things because of guys. So, are you satisfied?"

I consider her story for a moment. "No. I'm not."

She can't believe it. "Why not?"

"I won't be satisfied until you do something about Kevin. The fact that you've kept this proves that you like him. You've got me out there in a bikini giving swim lessons. I want you to put a little effort into Kevin."

For the first time, there's a crack in her armor. "Like what?" she asks.

"You could call him," I say, holding up my cell phone. "I'm sure you know the number."

Melanie shakes her head. "What would I say? 'Remember that lollipop you gave me in seventh grade? Guess what.'"

"Okay, probably not that. But you could invite him over to watch *Pirates of the Caribbean*."

"Cute. Very cute."

"Then don't call him. Just do *something*." I try to come up with an idea.

"What if he's at Michelle's party this week?"

This catches her interest. "Yeah?"

"You could . . . talk to him?"

She thinks this over for a moment. "I could do that."

"Maybe you could even . . . dance with him."

"You know I can't dance."

I crack a smile. "I even know the perfect song." I do my best LL Cool J impression.

> "*Lolli-lolli-pop-pop bopping down the block-block*
> *I've been loving you since Junior High School . . .*"

She slams me in the head with a pillow. "I can't believe you just sang that," she says.

"Or how about this one? '*Yo ho, yo ho, a pirate's life for me.*'"

"Now you've gone too far," she says. "You, you . . . mermaid liar!"

"Candy keeper!"

Just as we're each trying to keep a straight face and stare each other down, something catches our attention. On the TV some Josh Groban wannabe is absolutely butchering "You Raise Me Up." It is so terrible that we can't take our eyes off of it.

Suddenly it dawns on me why the show is so popular. Melanie is right, we all do stupid, incredibly embarrassing stuff. When we see other people do the same, it comforts us to know that we're not alone.

Ten

While Tragic Waters may be a somewhat pathetic destination for tourists, it turns out to be a pretty fun place to work. Surprisingly, I actually enjoy playing Eager Beaver. Of course, I could never admit this to Bec and Mel after being such a drama queen about it. But it's a blast dancing around as a cartoon character. You get to be goofy, and kids love you.

At least most kids do.

Right now, a little girl is eyeing me nervously while her mother tries to get her to pose for a picture.

"Please don't eat me, Mr. Beaver," she says with a gulp as I put my arm around her. She's scared, and it's hard to blame her. After all, she's five and there's a giant woodland creature with freakishly large buck teeth kneeling down beside her. Shouldn't she be scared?

But her mother has run out of patience. Sunburned and frazzled, she's just trying to make it to the end of the day. "Just shut up and smile!" she barks.

Now frightened of both the giant beaver and her mother, the girl grimaces just long enough so that it looks like a smile in the picture.

Ah, the sweet beauty of a family vacation.

We're at the end of what's called a "meet and greet." Three times a day we dance onstage to a few songs. Then we go out into the audience, shake hands with a bunch of kids, and pose for family pictures. (Most of which are much more pleasant than this one.)

The best part of being Eager Beaver is that unlike the contestants on *American Idol* who flame out in front of millions of people, I get to stay completely anonymous. No matter how silly or stupid I act, nobody knows that it's me inside the costume.

Don't get me wrong. The job also has its drawbacks. You don't really know what heat is until you've worn a fur costume in the middle of the Florida summer. One day I had my hair pulled back with a rubber band and the rubber actually melted into my ponytail. My mom had to pick the pieces out with a lice comb.

The other drawback is the parade.

This year is the park's fiftieth anniversary, so the parade has been renamed "The Golden Jamboree." It's really the same old parade, except the pirate float has been redecorated to look like a giant birthday cake. (Actually, it looks like a pirate ship with frosting, but at least they tried.)

During the parade, we're supposed to follow the cake and dance around to music played by a mini marching band. The guests follow along too, and the whole thing ends at (get ready to gag) the mermaid lagoon, where the mermaids are waiting. Then they have a firework show. (Notice I didn't say "fireworks" plural. They just shoot off one lousy firework. Disney World, this isn't.)

My problem is that I still haven't fully

gotten the hang of looking through those eye slits in the helmet. I keep slamming into the giant birthday cake float. One time I bounced off of it so hard that my tail wiped out two members of the band.

Today I march close to Grayson so he can make sure I don't wander off course. I also want to be with him when the parade ends because after work he is pulling off the greatest practical joke in history.

We're talking pure evil genius.

It all started the other day, when we were practicing our routine in the hallway outside the locker room. I did it totally wrong and fell smack on my butt right as Crystal and one of the mer-chicks walked by.

Rather than help me up, she just looked down, laughed, and made a totally rude comment to her friend. Already flustered from the fall, I just sat there and took it. Typical Plain Jane.

Grayson saw the whole thing and he was fuming. It got us talking, and I wound up telling him the whole Crystal-Jane saga. When I finished, he just smiled and asked me a simple question:

"Want to get even?"

I didn't even answer. I just smiled and nodded. He took over from there. For the past three days he's been writing incredibly romantic letters and slipping them into her locker. Then we hang out and watch her read them.

Every day she does the same thing. First she reads the letter. Then she grins from ear to ear, thinking about it. Finally, she looks around and tries to figure out which guy is her secret admirer.

Today Grayson is delivering his final one. He won't tell me what it says, but he promises that it's a winner.

I rush in from the parade and quickly switch into some street clothes. Then I head out to the hallway, where all the lockers are. Grayson is sitting at a table pretending to read the employee newsletter.

I sit down right next to him and pick up one too.

"Did I miss anything?"

"Nope," he says under his breath. "But she's coming right now." He nods down the hall, and I see Crystal walking our way with a big smile on her face.

Even though she just got out of the

water, she looks immaculate. Her makeup's perfect, and not a hair is out of place. I can't help but smile. It's just like my Bikini Jane moments. She's primped for this. She wants to look her best for this guy.

"You might want to get your camera phone," Grayson suggests. "To show the friends you told me about."

Great idea. I act like I'm making a call, and point the camera right at her locker. She opens it and beams, obviously thrilled to find yet another letter.

She looks both ways to see if anyone's watching. Then she starts reading, and I start taking pictures.

First her eyes open wide. Then her lips thin and whiten. She balls up the letter and throws it to the ground. My last shot is of her perfect little butt stomping out to the employee parking lot. She looks so mad that I almost feel sorry for her.

Almost.

Finally, when she's gone, I turn to Grayson. "What did you write?"

He nods over to the crumpled note on the floor.

"See for yourself."

I go over to the locker wall and pick the paper up off of the floor. As I read it, I start to laugh my butt off. It's perfect in its simplicity:

"Sorry, I thought this locker belonged to somebody else. Please ignore the last three notes."

Eleven

WELCOME TO JANE'S BEACH!

That's what it says on the sign that hangs above the door in my room. It used to say WELCOME TO JANUS BEACH, but that was before Becca and Melanie drove to Janus Beach, stole the sign, and painted an "E apostrophe" over the "U."

They gave it to me as a victory present after my big win at the state swim meet. Whenever I see the sign I think about how crazy it must have been at the scene of the crime. Master criminals, they are not.

The sign has a big picture of the Roman god Janus. According to the myth, Janus had two faces looking in opposite directions. Lately, I've been feeling a lot like him. It's not that I'm two-faced in the Crystal Gentry kind of way. But I definitely feel like I'm developing a split personality.

Sometimes, I'm Bikini Jane—a confident girl who struts around in a two-piece and feels more and more at ease flirting with a twelfth-degree hottie. At other times, I'm Plain Jane—a shy girl who waddles around in a beaver costume and is getting used to little kids yanking her oversize tail.

The weird part is that I like both.

Right now I'm in Bikini Jane mode heading over to Alex's. Despite the hair scrunching, makeup, and sense of confidence, I don't feel like a phony when I'm with him.

I never say anything that I don't mean, and I don't play games like pretending to be an airhead. (I hate it when girls do that.) The only bad part is the lie I told him about being a mermaid. But that was more a panic thing than a phony thing. (At least I hope it was.) I'm confident around Alex, but it's still me.

I think it helps that all of our time

together has been in the pool, where I'm already sure of myself. When I'm at a swim meet, I feel like everyone else is swimming for second place. But when it comes to guys, I've always been the runner-up. I'm the one they come to with their problems, or (even worse) to talk to about the girls they do like. But Alex has changed that.

It's not like anything is happening between us. So far, it's just flirting. But it feels like something *could* happen. And that's a big step.

"What are we doing today?" he asks as we get into the pool.

"I'm going to teach you the back float," I tell him as I get behind him. "All you've got to do is lean back."

The back float is probably the hardest thing for adults to learn because they can't see the water until they're in it.

He's uneasy at first, but then he finally starts coming back. I catch him and help him ease into the water.

"You're doing great," I tell him. "Just try to relax and let the water hold you up."

I move my hand from his shoulders down the center of his back until I'm holding him up with just the tips of my fingers. I try to keep my focus on the lesson, but I have to admit, it's pretty sexy.

Everything is perfect.

Then it starts to rain.

By the time we make it inside the house, it's pouring. I look over at Alex, and he looks happier than I've ever seen him.

"Guess the lesson's over," he says.

"Looks like it," I say.

Then he catches me off guard. "Want to watch a movie?"

"It's nine in the morning," I say. "I don't think there are any theaters open."

"I know one," he says with a smile. He leads me upstairs to where his dad has built the most unbelievable home theater.

"Although I officially hate the house," he says, "I have to admit, Dad got this room right. It's got THX surround sound and a sixty-inch flat-screen monitor. All you've got to do is pick the movie."

(Just for the record, I am technically counting this as date number one.)

We dig through a stack of DVDs to look for anything that we might like. Apparently his father and stepmother are really into war movies, Westerns, and Pilates exercise routines. Finally, he comes across a possibility.

"Do you like horror movies?" he asks.

I scrunch my face. I hate horror movies. I never watch them. I usually don't even like people who like them. But it's our first date, so I'll agree to anything.

I rearrange my face. "Sure, which one is it?"

He holds the DVD, and I start to laugh. It's *Blue Crush*.

"That's about girls who surf. That's not a horror movie."

He looks at the cover. "It is if you're scared of the water."

As he puts it in, I ask him a question. "I get that your dad likes war movies and Westerns. And I'm guessing your mother—"

"Stepmother," he corrects instantly.

"Excuse me, stepmother, likes to work out. But which one bought *Blue Crush*?"

He thinks about it for a moment and has a perplexed look. "I don't know. But either way, it kind of creeps me out."

He grabs the remote and we sit

together—not touching, but together on the couch. As the opening credits roll, I ask myself, *What would Bikini Jane do?*

I take a quick breath, reach over, and slide my hand in his. It's electric and it's thrilling. He doesn't look over at me or even say a word. But he wraps his fingers between mine, and I melt. (*Blue Crush* is now my favorite movie.)

Since we've both seen the movie before, we spend a lot of time making fun of it. He even does a hilarious impression of Kate Bosworth at the end of the movie when she rides out of the last big wave and pumps her fist in the air.

By the time the movie's over, the rain has stopped and both of us have to get going to work.

"Thanks for the movie," I say. "It was fun."

"Yeah," he says. "Horrifying, but fun."

He walks me to my car, and we hold hands the whole way. My heart is racing. All I can think about is whether we're going to kiss.

A couple of times it looks like he's going to make a move, but he doesn't. I pretty much give up on it once I fasten my seat belt.

Then he leans in through the window and starts to give me a kiss. It catches me completely off guard. In fact, it catches me so off guard that my foot slips off the brake.

That's when I run over his foot.

Twelve

"Let me get this straight," Becca says as she dips a chip into some guacamole. "He kissed you. And, instead of kissing him back, you ran over him with your car?"

"Just his foot," I say, wishing it weren't true. "But, yes. That's what happened."

Melanie fights the urge to laugh. "Well, that was an interesting choice."

"It was just an accident," I offer in my own defense. "It sounds way worse than it was."

Melanie nods. "I hope so, because it sounds awful."

It really does sound worse than it was. Alex wasn't hurt at all, and we both laughed about it. The lousy part is that I really wanted to kiss him back. With the movie and the hand-holding, everything was perfect. Now I don't know if I'll get another chance. In two weeks he'll officially be a Pollywog and I won't have an excuse to keep coming over.

"Tonight I want you to study the girls at the party," Becca says. "Notice how none of them run over the boys they like."

I can already tell I'll be hearing about this for the rest of my life.

Tonight we're going to a party at Michelle Nagler's house. To me, parties are like albums. Some are loud. Some are alternative. And some should come with a Parental Advisory label for explicit content. Michelle's parties are always good— kind of like a soundtrack album—with a little something for everybody.

Bec and Mel have decided the party will be the next step in the evolution of Bikini Jane. We're going to watch the couples in action and study all the methods girls use to attract guys.

First, though, we had to stop at Mama Taco's to fuel up. Now that we've polished off a plate of chicken nachos, a pitcher of Diet Coke, and who knows how many baskets of chips and guac, we're ready to go. Rather than drive, we just walk along the beach toward Michelle's house.

I take off my sandals and walk barefoot in the cool, damp sand. I can't imagine what it's like to go to a high school that isn't near the ocean. The beach is the epicenter of our social universe. It's where we lie out and watch the surf boys with ripped abs. It's where we play beach volleyball and touch football. And it's where we have most of our parties.

On a Friday or Saturday night, all you need to do is walk along the tide and follow the music. As we get close to Michelle's, we can already hear the steady thump of Green Day.

"Don't forget our deal, Melanie."

"What deal?" Becca asks.

I throw an arm around Mel's shoulder. "She said that if Kevin is here, she's going to make her move."

Becca smiles. "Well, all right, Mama."

"Actually, that's not what I said," Melanie interjects. "I was just trying to get her to shut up so I could watch *American Idol*."

Typical Melanie. But I'm not going to let her get away with it.

"That's right," I answer. "We were watching *Idol*. What was that song that guy sang? Now I remember."

"Lolli-lolli pop-pop bopping down the block-block—"

Melanie cuts me off. "Okay. I'll talk to him."

Mel tenses up as we do a lap around the party. But she relaxes when there's no sign of him. Considering he's six four, he's usually pretty hard to miss.

"Damn," she says with a big smile on her face. "And I thought tonight was going to be the night."

The party is already going strong. We stop inside to say hello to Michelle and to grab some drinks. Then we head out back and climb the wooden stairs that lead to a second-story deck. It has an amazing view of the ocean, which is why Michelle's parents built it. It's also the perfect place to spy on everybody, which is why we're up here.

We settle in for an observation session. But as I scan the crowd, I can't find anything worth studying.

"What am I looking for?" I ask as I scan the crowd.

"Just pointers," Becca says. "Watch how the girls work it, and learn from their mistakes."

Over the next half hour, Bec and Mel identify a variety of girl species. The whole thing sounds like something on Animal Planet except with cheerleaders instead of wildebeests.

"Look over there," Becca says, motioning to a bubbly sophomore laughing a little too much at some guy's jokes. "Classic Desperate Girl. You definitely do not want to be her."

"Absolutely," Melanie says. "Notice the clothes, one size too tight—it makes her boobs look bigger, but her butt looks chunky too. And notice the glassy eyes. She's already drunk."

Becca continues. "She'll find a guy tonight, but it will be for one night only. It's like that junk on eBay that no one really wants. The auction's started, and she'll go to whoever bothers to put in a bid."

I love her to death, but Becca can be one cold girl.

A few minutes later, Melanie picks another one out of the herd. She nods over to where a guy and a girl are talking. Actually, only the guy is talking.

"Check out Pouty Girl," Mel says. "For some unknown reason, guys find that attractive. Notice the lower lip, the eyes— they're sexy, not angry."

"Right," Becca says, taking over. "And check out the physical contact. Her hand is on his leg. That's the bait. That's the way she keeps him there."

"You guys are twisted, you know that."

They smile like I've just given them a great compliment. As we scan for the next subject, I recognize a familiar but surprising face: Grayson.

"What's he doing here?"

"Who?" asks Becca.

"Grayson. The guy I work with at Magic Waters."

Melanie grins. "Is he the one who wrote the fake love letters to Crystal?"

I laugh just thinking of it. "That's him."

"Grayson!" I call down. He turns around and smiles when he sees me. I signal him to come up and join us on the deck.

As he walks up, Melanie makes a surprising comment. "Why didn't you mention he was so cute?"

This is surprising because it never occurred to me. I've never thought about his appearance. He's just my buddy Grayson.

"What are you doing here, Platypus Man?" I say as he reaches up. "I thought this party was strictly RBH."

He gives me a confused look. "RBH?"

"Ruby Beach High."

"That explains the secret handshake at the door," he says with a laugh. "Do I need some kind of party hall pass or something?"

"Nah, I'll vouch for you," I tell him. I turn to the girls. "Grayson goes to Fletcher."

"That's cool," Melanie chimes in. "How'd you hear about the party? Do you know Michelle?"

"Yeah," he says. "We're pretty close, actually. We're in the same church group."

"You got here just in time," Becca says. "We're on a fact-finding mission, trying to help our—"

"Becca!" I protest. I don't want her telling this stuff to him. She couldn't care less. She just keeps going.

"Trying to help our friend Jane study the great mysteries of teen mating. You see she's got her eye on someone but isn't sure how to make the first move."

Apparently I have no right to privacy.

"Is it anyone I know?" Grayson asks. "Maybe Krys the choreographer?"

"None of us know him," Melanie says.

Becca nods. "Supposedly he's gorgeous and at constant risk of drowning. Jane's giving him swim lessons."

"Which is supposed to be a secret," I remind them.

"Yeah," Becca says. "Should've thought about that before you told us."

"Anyway, we could use a male perspective in our search," Melanie adds completely out of nowhere.

No, we couldn't.

But it's too late. Grayson's already smiling and joining our expedition.

"Any way I can help," he offers.

"First, we've got some questions and we'd like answers," Melanie says. "For example, what's with the Pouty Girl thing? Why do guys like that?"

Grayson mulls this over for a moment. "That's a hard one. I guess I'd have to say— I don't know."

Becca raises her eyebrows. "That doesn't really help us."

"It should," Grayson says. "The biggest problem girls have understanding guys is that you think too much. Guys are not that complicated. You're always looking for some deep answer or reason for how we act. But the truth is that about half the time, 'I don't know' is all we've got."

Melanie shakes her head. "That would drive me crazy. How can you possibly live that way?"

He smiles. "I don't know."

We all nod. A guy's perspective might help after all.

Grayson's sense of humor is an instant hit with Becca and especially with Melanie, who's normally a little shy around new people.

He takes the Animal Planet concept one step further and does his analysis like the Croc Hunter, complete with a perfect Australian accent.

This continues until the music changes and Usher comes on. Without warning, Becca turns into a superfreak. When the right song comes on, Bec just drops what she's doing and starts to dance.

She's an incredible dancer. She claims it has something to do with gyrating her hips on the offbeat and moving her shoulders to the beat. (Whatever it is, Mel and I can't do it.)

Usher is one of her favorites.

Within seconds of hitting the dance floor, three guys materialize, each trying to dance with her.

"That's pretty amazing," Grayson says as he digests the whole thing.

"That's Bec for you," I tell him.

We all start to move to the music a bit. I close my eyes and feel the sea breeze blow over me. It feels really great. Then I hear Grayson ask, "Wanna dance?"

Before I can say, "Sure," Melanie beats

me to the punch and says, "Love to."

Just like that, they are out on the dance floor. This is the same girl who just a couple of days ago said that she never dances. The one who's waited four years to act on a crush. Now she's out there getting busy.

Grayson is really into it too. Most guys I know can't dance. They either play air guitar and lip-synch, or they bounce all over the place like the whole world's a mosh pit. But he's got some skillful moves. Apparently, all that platypus dancing has come in handy.

As they dance, I realize that this is the first time I've seen him in regular clothes. Usually he's dressed like a platypus. When he's not, he's in the Tragic Waters shorts and T-shirt that we wear under the costumes.

Now, though, he's wearing a pair of cargo shorts and a polo shirt. With no bandanna on his head, it turns out he's got a mop of cool surfer hair.

Melanie's right. Somehow, without my knowing it, Grayson turned out to be cute. Really cute.

It's really a crappy time to realize it,

because he's dancing closer and closer to my best friend on the planet.

Now, here's the totally freaky part.

I'M JEALOUS.

I have absolutely no idea why. I've never thought about Grayson that way. I would love for Melanie to find a boyfriend. And I just got kissed by the hottest guy I've ever known.

But I'm mad jealous.

Just when I thought my life could not get more complicated.

Thirteen

The music has shifted from Usher to OutKast to U2, with Melanie and Grayson showing no signs of letting up. (My jealousy factor, though, has steadily climbed.) Becca, meanwhile, is scamming on some guy I vaguely recognize from student government. Suddenly, I'm the odd one out.

I turn to Becca. "I've got to go."

"What?"

I can tell she's surprised, and in a way so am I. It's just that watching the two of them dancing is kind of making me nuts. And since I don't want to be nuts in front of my two best friends and a guy I work with every day, I figure the best thing to do is bolt.

"I've got swim practice in the morning." (My classic lame excuse.)

Becca shrugs and turns back to the boy. I wave at the dancing duo and make a quick exit. I'm already down on the beach when Grayson and Melanie catch up to me.

"Are you leaving?" he asks.

"Yeah. I've got to get to bed. I have swim practice in the morning. You guys should dance some more. You're really good at it."

Apparently I say it kind of pissy, because it really ticks Melanie off. "Why are you being such a B?" (We have a strict rule that even when we're pissed we never call each other a bitch. B is as far as we'll go.)

"I don't know what you're talking about. I've got swim practice in the morning."

Grayson looks a little disappointed, and I worry that I'm overreacting.

"Do you want me to walk you home?"

Melanie is instantly wounded, but he quickly recovers. "I mean us. Do you want us to walk you home? If you want to, Melanie?"

"No," I say. "It's just a few blocks. I've got to get to sleep. You guys have fun."

Melanie doesn't even respond. She's pissed. Grayson's just confused.

"Okay. I'll see you at work tomorrow."

"See you tomorrow."

I give a little smile, wave good-bye, and start down the beach. After a couple of blocks, the music fades and all I hear is the surf.

A blast of salt air washes over me, and I try to understand what just happened. For some strange reason I was jealous of Grayson dancing with Melanie. I don't know why.

Whatever the reason, my hasty exit messed up what was going on with Melanie and Grayson. He seemed clueless, but I could tell she was into him. Now she's pissed because I upset it. I hate to think it, but maybe that's why I did it. Maybe I wanted to get Grayson's focus off Melanie and on me.

That would mean that while Bikini Jane is hot for Alex, Plain Jane has a crush on Grayson. It doesn't seem possible. I've always been monogamous. (Technically, you can't be monogamous if you don't have a boyfriend. But I've always kept my obsessive-compulsive secret crushes to one guy at a time.)

By the time I reach First Street, I try to put it all out of my mind. I turn away from the beach and walk the last couple of blocks to my house. The house is quiet, but luckily I find the two people who best know how to get through such dilemmas.

Ben and Jerry.

I get a pint of Chunky Monkey from the freezer and make myself comfortable on the couch. Since Mom's asleep and everyone else is gone, I have complete control of the remote. I channel surf until I come across *Charlie's Angels: Full Throttle*. (I swear, it is on HBO every single night.) It's mindless, and mindless is exactly what I need.

Besides, it's good to see three girls working together with no petty jealousy. I could learn something from them.

Even though I've seen it who knows how many times, I catch something I hadn't noticed before. During the opening credits, Cameron Diaz wears a beaver costume. How about that, me and Cameron D?

I never got to be Cameron back in middle school when the first movie came out. We used to play *Charlie's Angels* all the time and we'd fight over who got to be which angel. Crystal was one of us then, so I usually got stuck being Bosley and Charlie. (The curse of the flat-chested strikes again.)

Halfway through the movie, my dad gets home from a late shift at the firehouse. Even when he's exhausted, he can't help but tell jokes.

"You look just like my daughter. Used to hang around here all the time until we got her a car. Haven't seen her since."

"Gee, Dad, that's funny every time."

He quickly sizes up the situation. "Chunky Monkey and crappy movie. This can't be good. Boy problems?"

"No problems. Go to bed, Dad."

"I would, except I happen to love this movie soooo much."

"You love *Charlie's Angels?*"

"No, no, no. Not just *Charlie's Angels*," he corrects me. "*Charlie's Angels: Full Throttle.*"

I can't help but laugh.

Only my dad would know right away that it's the sequel. He's a movie freak.

When he's on duty and can't leave the station, he watches movies. He and the guys on his truck can go for hours reciting their favorite lines.

He squeezes into the love seat next to me even though there's a perfectly good—and empty—couch. "What scene is it?"

"It's *Charlie's Angels*, Dad. Does it matter?"

"Aren't you Little Miss Art Snob? *Charlie's Angels: Full Throttle*—or *CAFT* as the boys in the station house like to call it—happens to be an important piece of art."

I give him a look that says I know he's full of it.

"Young women such as you dismiss it as a treatise on girl power."

"No one says 'girl power' anymore, Dad."

"Whereas young men see it merely as a good excuse to watch full-figured women in hand-to-hand combat."

"No one says 'full-figured,' either."

"But for men of culture such as myself, *Charlie's Angels: Full Throttle*—"

"You mean *CAFT*?"

"Of course—*CAFT* is purely political satire, a searing analysis of our government and Constitution."

He just sits there and waits for me to take the bait. The problem is that I can't ignore it, and that will only encourage him to do it again next time.

"Okay, I give. Tell me how it's a searing analysis of our form of government?"

"I'm glad you asked. You see, the three angels represent our three branches of government. Cameron Diaz is the well meaning but somewhat dim-witted leader—obviously modeled after recent presidents. Meanwhile, Lucy Liu represents the restrained intelligence of the Supreme Court—that's why they always dress her in black, to symbolize judges' robes. And, finally, Drew Barrymore is clearly a symbol of the drunken promiscuity that is the United States Congress."

He says it so convincingly that if you weren't paying attention, you'd think it was true.

"And this is why you watch it?"

"Hell no," he shoots back. "I watch it to see Demi Moore in a bikini. Hubba hubba."

That's my dad in a nutshell.

I roll my eyes and threaten to flick a

spoonful of ice cream at him. Now that he's cheered me up, he gets up to go to sleep. He gives me a kiss on the forehead.

"About whatever brought on the Chunky Monkey/crappy-movie combo, you do know that if you want to talk about anything, all you have to do is walk down the hall?"

"I know. I know. I can come to you anytime."

He flashes me an appalled look. "I didn't mean me. I was going to say you can wake your mother. But that's sweet that you thought I was going to say me."

I threaten another flick, and he heads down the hall. I almost make it to the end of the movie and head for bed around two in the morning.

I send a quick apology e-mail to Melanie, and the last thing I see before I fall asleep is the picture of Janus on the sign in my room. One man with two faces looking in different directions.

I know just how he feels.

Fourteen

When I wake up in the morning, I check my computer and see that Melanie is already online. (Her icon is the picture of Spider-Man hanging upside down kissing Kirsten Dunst.) I decide to test the waters and IM her.

SwimFast203: Are you still talking to me? :(
(There's a long pause.)
MrsMaguire: Give me a reason I should.
SwimFast203: 7 years BFF vs. 10 minutes drama queen.
(Another pause)
MrsMaguire: You're lucky I'm generous.

SwimFast203: :)

SwimFast203: You like him, don't you?

MrsMaguire: Doesn't matter. He's hot for someone.

SwimFast203: Michelle Nagler?

MrsMaguire: No, idiot! You!

SwimFast203: Impossible!!!!! Did he tell you that?

MrsMaquire: He didn't have to.

SwimFast203: Then why do you think that?

MrsMaguire: Well, he didn't offer to walk me home.

SwimFast203: LOL. I've got to go to work.

MrsMaguire: C U L8R

SwimFast203: Ciao.

Melanie can't be right about Grayson. I've worked with him almost a month now, and I've never gotten that vibe. Besides, I'm way too focused on another hottie at the moment.

I have no idea what's going to happen between Alex and me. I thought I did while we were holding hands and watching *Blue Crush*. But then there was the whole botched-kiss-run-over-his-foot thing.

As I drive over to his house, I try to brace myself for what his reaction to yesterday might be. I don't know what the face-to-face equivalent of Radio Karma is, but when he opens the door I think his expression should give me a hint about our future.

I knock and take an anxious breath.

"Hi! You must be Jane."

Not what I was expecting. The voice is shrill and ear-shattering. I look up and see a woman I can only assume is Alex's stepmother. I say "assume" because she says, "I just absolutely insist that you call me Josie. Like the Pussycats."

She's one of those grown-ups who is desperate to feel cool and hip around kids. (That's what I love about my dad. His jokes are so dopey and uncool that kids actually do like to be around him.) Within seconds, Josie is blabbing away like she's one of the girls.

I'm with Alex: I can't stand her.

She's a "Stacey's Mom" wannabe. Her face has had too many BOTOX treatments, collagen injections, and chemical peels. Not to mention a religious commitment to tanning beds. Her breasts defy gravity, and her hair has not seen its original color during my lifetime. (Secretly, this woman is what I'm hoping Crystal will become.)

She leads me to Alex, who is in the kitchen.

"Here's our little Pollywog," she says, managing to be supportive and demeaning at the same time.

"How's your foot?" I ask when I reach him in the kitchen.

"Fine," he says curtly.

At first, I get the sense that he's giving me the cold shoulder. (Can you blame him? He kissed me, and I tried to hobble him.) It's not until we're outside and in the pool that I realize the cold shoulder is directed at her and not me. (Thank God.)

There's no way for us to resume flirting, because Josie has decided to lie out and work on her tan. (Her next shade will be charcoal.) Her bikini is smaller than mine, and when she lies on her stomach, her butt does a wicked impression of cottage cheese.

Be careful, Bikini Jane. This could be your future.

Alex and I focus on the swimming. (We also try to avert our eyes from Josie at all times.)

I'm amazed at how much better he's gotten. I'd like to think that it's my teaching. But it's more a matter of his determination. When the lesson's done, he walks me to the car. It's the first time we've been alone the whole morning.

"Isn't she the worst?" he says under his breath.

"She's pretty dreadful," I reply.

"How my father could leave my mother to marry her is beyond me."

I can tell this really bothers him. And it should. So when we reach the car, I try to lighten the mood. I do my best Coach Latham impression: "Pretty soon you're going to have to take your swim test," I tell him. "That's when we'll separate the little boys from the little Pollywogs."

"Bring it on!" he says. There's that smile again. The one I see when I close my eyes.

This time I make sure the car is in park, in case he decides to try another lean-in and kiss. Just when I think he might, Josie walks around from the back.

"It was nice to meet you, *dawg*." (She's watched way too many episodes of MTV *Cribs*.) "Peace out."

Alex and I can't help but bust out laughing. Still, I wave and shout back, "Peace out, Mrs. Walker."

"Now, now, girlfriend, call me Josie."

"Peace out, Josie."

By the time I'm out of the driveway, I'm laughing so hard that tears are rolling down my face.

The weirdness of the day continues at Magic Waters. Grayson seems like he's acting different. I don't know if he is because I bolted the party and hurt his feelings. Or, maybe he's acting normal but I *think* he's acting different because Melanie said he likes me and now *I'm* acting different.

I have enough trouble reading someone under normal circumstances. But it's nearly impossible to read someone who is dressed like a giant platypus.

After my shift I can't track down either Mel or Becca. I decide to hit the pool at the Y and put in some work. One of the advantages of giving lessons is that I have my own set of keys. The pool is all mine.

The moon is full, and the water is inviting. I just hit the water and pound away. When I compete, I try to outthink the girls I'm up against. But the key to training is shutting off your mind and becoming a machine.

With each stroke I clear my mind just a little bit more. No more Bikini Jane or Plain Jane. Stroke after stroke. No Alex or Grayson. No Becca or Melanie. Just me and the pool.

I'm in full machine mode until something catches my eye in the middle of a flip turn. It's a person watching me. I stop and take off my goggles. My vision's a little blurry, but I realize it's my mother.

"What are you doing here?"

She looks down at me, concerned. "I was looking for you."

Panic. "Is something wrong? Is Dad okay?"

"Everyone's fine. I was just worried. Becca and Melanie called. You didn't answer your cell. No one knew where you were."

"Sorry, I can't hear the cell in the water."

I still don't get the sudden urgency. It's not like I missed my curfew.

"Do you know what time it is?"

"I don't know. Nine thirty, ten."

She laughs. "It's after midnight, Janey."

Okay, maybe I did miss my curfew. But it can't be midnight. I look at the clock on the pool deck and see that she's right.

"How long have you been here?"

"I don't know. But it's probably time that I got out of the water."

She laughs some more. "I think so."

I climb out and towel off. I feel exhausted and great at the same time. It's the kind of relaxed that only comes when you're totally spent.

I can tell that Mom's not mad about my being late, but she still looks concerned. "Baby, is everything okay?"

I think about it for a moment. I've got a guy I like. A job that's fun. And, I'm hopeful about getting a scholarship to a school I'd love.

"No, Mom. Everything's better than okay. Everything's great."

"That's an answer a mother wants to hear."

I lock up the pool area, and we walk toward the parking lot. I look at her and realize that she's actually prettier than Alex's stepmom. She dresses nice, but not trendy. She's got some gray and a few saggy spots, but all where they're supposed to be. Secretly, this is what I've always dreamed I'd become.

"How'd you know where to find me?"

She looks at me like I'm insane. "Are you kidding? I'm your mother. I knew you'd be here."

"How?"

"Because it's where you feel the most comfortable."

I look back at the pool through the chain-link fence. The water sparkles from the full moon, and the smell of chlorine fills the air. I realize that my mother is pretty smart. This *is* where I'm most comfortable.

I call to her as she gets into her car.

"You're never going to call me or any of my friends 'dawg,' are you?"

"No," she says. "I figure if I teach English, the least I can do is speak it. We'll leave the nonsense to your father."

Fifteen

I'm in my deepest sleep in recent memory. My late-night endurance swim has knocked me out cold, and it feels great. The only problem is that now I'm battling a new nightmare. This time there's no giant beaver at school. Instead, I'm being tormented by a giant Kendra at my bedside.

"Wake up. It's the phone."

I slowly process what she's saying and realize that it isn't a dream. It's the real Kendra.

"What?" I answer. (Actually, I'm sure it comes out more like "whuuu," but in my head, it started out as "what.")

"You . . . have . . . a . . . phone . . . call."

I wipe some sleep from my eyes and try to focus on her, the clock, anything. It's useless. Then, just as I'm about to ignore her and go back to sleep, I hear four magic words.

"Some guy named Alex."

That wakes me up faster than five venti cappuccinos.

"Alex?"

I snatch the cordless right out of her hand and quickly cover the mouthpiece. Still a little disoriented, I try to get my bearings. I have one key question for her.

"Do I look okay?"

"It's the *phone,* Einstein. You look like a supermodel."

"Right," I say. "Now get out."

She shakes her head and leaves the room. I take a deep breath and try my best to sound coherent.

"Hello."

"Jane? This is Alex—Alex Walker—from swim lessons. I hope I didn't wake you up."

"Are you kidding?" I say. "I've been up for hours."

Suddenly, I wonder how he got my phone number. I never gave it to him. He had to look it up. Good sign.

"I know we don't have a lesson scheduled for today, but I wanted to talk to you."

"Sure," I say. "What's up? Is something wrong?"

"About yesterday, with my stepmother . . . she's so pathetic. . . . And that whole 'dawg' thing when you drove off . . . I don't know where *that* came from. . . . I'm just really embarrassed."

"It was pretty bad," I answer truthfully. "But you don't have to apologize for it."

There's a long silence on the other end. "The thing is . . . I wanted to talk to you about something . . . but I couldn't do it. Not with her . . . hanging out by the pool."

"Sure, what's up?"

There's a long pause.

"I was wondering if you'd like to go out . . . you know . . . with me . . . tonight."

For a second I can't even breathe. Everything stands still, and there's total quiet except for a songbird outside my window.

"That's not against some YMCA rule, is

it? For you to go on a date with someone you're teaching."

If so, then I'm quitting the Y. Of course, so far, I've only taught preschoolers and elementary kids. So it hasn't really come up.

"No. There's no rule. That I know of."

"Great," he says. "So, would you like to go?"

Suddenly it dawns on me that I haven't answered him yet. It's way too early for Bikini Jane cool, so I just blurt it out.

"Are you kidding?! I mean . . . well, I mean . . . of course. I'd love to."

There's a brief pause on the other side, and I worry that my eagerness has scared him off.

"Great. I work at the club until seven. How about seven thirty? I'll pick you up at your house."

"Perfect," I answer. "Seven thirty."

We talk for a few more minutes, and I give him directions to my house. After I hang up I check the phone three times to make sure that the dial tone is really there and there's no way he can hear me. Then I bury my face in my pillow and scream at the top of my lungs.

It's not that I've never been on a date before. It's just that they've usually been more friend-friend dates for events like Homecoming. This certainly jumps to the top of my lifetime social history.

I call Becca and Melanie as I drive in to Magic Waters. They're beyond excited, and Becca's already trying to figure out a way the two of them can spy on the date while it's in progress.

Work is a total blur. My mind is way too focused on tonight. After the parade, I rush home and get there just after six. I've got almost an hour and a half to get ready and I plan on using every second. I come in through the kitchen, where my mother is making her famous spaghetti sauce.

"Are you home for dinner?" she says with a smile.

I stop and try not to grin from ear to ear.

"I have plans tonight."

She shakes in some garlic powder. It smells great. "Where are you girls off to this time?"

I can't fight the grin anymore. "Not with Bec and Melanie. I have a date. With a boy. An extremely, unbelievably cute boy. He will be coming here tonight. To pick me up and take me out."

She slaps the garlic powder down so hard that the bottle almost breaks. She tries not to look too excited.

"What boy?"

"His name is Alex Walker."

"Do I know him?"

"No. I've been giving him swim lessons."

"What is he? Eight?" I turn around and see Kendra walking into the kitchen. Of course this is the time my entire family decides to be home.

I give her a defiant look. "No, he's seventeen."

She smirks. "A seventeen-year-old boy who can't swim. Sounds like a winner." She reaches over to dab a fingertip into the sauce. Mom slaps it away. "At least that explains why you've been stealing my bikinis. I was beginning to worry."

I didn't realize she knew about them. I quickly try to change the subject. "Anyway, to answer the original question: No, I will not be staying for dinner tonight. Now, if you don't mind, I have to get ready."

I rush upstairs and get busy. First I take a shower and try to get all the flecks of beaver helmet out of my hair.

Next I try to figure out what to wear. Instead of cool and casual—which is what I'm looking for—all I seem to find is dull and drab. I'm about to have a panic attack when Kendra comes into my room. Just as I go to ask her what's up, I realize why she's here.

"Mom sent you, didn't she? She sees this as a chance to bond."

"You got it." At least Kendra's honest.

She pauses for a moment and then looks me in the eye. "But that doesn't mean I wouldn't have stopped by anyway."

This makes me smile.

She looks over at the clothes I've laid out on the bed and reacts like those people who are about to eat worms on *Fear Factor*.

"You can't wear any of that," she says, pointing a finger at my clothes like they were somehow contagious.

Like I said, she's honest.

"I know."

Kendra thinks some more. "So is the guy you're going out with the one in the picture in your drawer?"

I'd taken the picture of Alex off my mirror and put it in my drawer. I give her a *What were you doing in my drawer?* look.

She's unfazed.

"I'm sorry, where did you find my bikinis?"

I think this over for a moment. "That's fair."

She opens the drawer and pulls out the picture. "He is cute. I'll give you that."

I decide to go for broke. "Cute enough that you'd let me borrow some clothes?"

"I don't think Brad Pitt's cute enough for that," she says.

"What if I told you that you're the reason I'm doing this?" I ask.

"What are you talking about?" she asks.

"The last time you came home from school," I say, trying to jog her memory. "When you dumped me at the mall so you could hang out with Erik."

"Oh yeah," she says, smiling at the memory.

"Right before you abandoned me, you gave me some good advice. You told me to make the most of this summer. That it should be the best three months of my life. That's what led to all this."

Kendra smiles, and I think it's sincere. "You see why I try not to be nice," she says. "I do something nice and what's my reward. Now I've got to let you borrow my clothes."

"Thank you, thank you, thank you!"

"But no shoes," she says, coming back to earth.

This totally changes the evening. Kendra's got college clothes—a little less fabric, a lot more sex appeal. I flip through her closet, but I don't even know where to begin.

"Try the light blue babydoll top with the cropped jeans."

I pull them out and hold them up together. "You think?" I ask skeptically.

She nods. "Let's just say that I've had some luck with that combination."

I think about this for a moment. "You have cleaned them since then, haven't you?"

"Just try them on, smart-ass."

I put them on and when I look in the mirror, I'm amazed by what I see. It's cute and sexy at the same time. (God, wouldn't I love that to be a term used to describe me.)

"Thank you."

"I want them back tomorrow. And dry cleaned."

"Whatever you say."

I go back to my room and manage to finish my hair and makeup exactly by seven. I take a deep breath and try to relax for a second. That's when I go to my bedroom window to look for his car and I see something that gets rid of any calm I may have—my dad's truck.

I hurry into the family room.

"Dad, what are you doing here? I thought you were working tonight."

"I got someone to cover," he says, flashing a big smile. "You didn't think I'd miss this, did you?"

Sixteen

"And you call yourself a mother?"

I shoot her a long, cold look. She'd sold me out and phoned my dad at the fire-house. Just so that he can do his handshake thing.

This routine started when Kendra went to her first boy-girl dance. It has carried through for the many boys who have ever come to pick her up as well as those few who've done so for me.

Before any first date, the boy has to meet Dad face-to-face. He looms over them and gives them that big fireman hand-shake. The one they use to pull people from burning buildings. All he does is smile, but the message is clear: "Be good to my girl. Or else."

There's a knock at the door, and I go to open it. Kendra reaches over and stops me.

"No way. You'll look too eager," she tells me. "Go back to your room. I'll answer."

I grab her arm. "No way." I notice the bare midriff and the short shorts. "You'll look too Kendra."

Mom just shakes her head and goes to the door and lets him in. I'm sure we look like idiots all clumped together in the front room. But if we do, he doesn't seem to react.

I introduce him to everyone, and he's great with them. He even handles Dad's handshake without being intimidated. (Years of tennis have given him a strong handshake.)

He scores major points by not rushing out the door. Instead, he sits in the living room and talks for a few minutes so my parents can get to know him.

"So, Mr. Quincy, Jane told me that you two like to watch documentaries together," he says, recalling our very first conversation.

Dad actually smiles. "I didn't know she

felt that way. We'll have to watch more."

"I only bring it up because my mother makes documentaries," Alex says. "Maybe you've seen one of them."

"What type does she do?" Dad asks.

"She did this show on the History Channel called *Hands on History*. With the guy learning about how products have evolved over the years."

"That's a good show," he says. "There's one about Louisville Sluggers." Dad's so excited that he's forgotten to be intimidating.

"That's the one," Alex says proudly. "That's my mom's show."

"Tell her that she's got a fan," Dad says.

Alex turns to my mother. "And Jane says you're an English teacher. That's my favorite subject. I'm even thinking about majoring in English."

Mom deals with a lot of kids, so I can tell she wants to make sure that he's not feeding her a line.

"Really? Who's your favorite author?" she asks, always the teacher.

"Steinbeck," he answers. "I especially like *The Grapes of Wrath*."

Unbelievable. That's mom's favorite book. She's sold. "Good answer. I like him too."

Leave it to Kendra to break the moment. "So what does she say about me?"

He smiles and answers. "Actually, she's never mentioned you."

Everybody laughs—even Kendra. I suggest that we should get going. As I leave, my mom flashes me a sly grin and nods her approval. I can't help but smile back.

"That was incredible," I say, nodding toward the house. "I think they're ready to adopt you."

He smiles. "After a couple of weeks with Josie, you really begin to appreciate quality adults."

He's the total gentleman and opens the car door for me. Then he gets in and asks, "Where would you like to go? I figure you know the town better."

"There is this one place," I say, unsure. "I don't know if you like Mexican, but it's called Mama Taco's and it's right on the beach."

"Are we dressed okay?"

I laugh at the idea of Mama Taco's having

any dress code. "Their policy is pretty much, 'No shirt, no shoes, no problem.'"

"Sounds like my kind of place," he says.

I really do like Mama Taco's. But I have a slight ulterior motive. When we walk into the restaurant, we walk right past a table where Becca and Melanie are already eating. Becca winks as we pass by, and Melanie pretends to fan herself with her menu.

Everything about the night is great— except for one thing. We hardly talk. And when we do, it's kind of nothing stuff, like about Mexican food or the decorations on the wall.

I've never felt so uncomfortable.

I blame it on our little Animal Planet mission at the beach party. We studied so many different types of girls and their behavior that now I don't know how to act or what to say.

Finally our food's ready and at least we have an excuse for the pauses. I'm having my regular, chicken nachos, while he's got a taco platter. He likes it, but I can tell he doesn't love it. I should have thought of a better place.

Melanie gives me a look as she and Becca go into the bathroom. After a few moments, I excuse myself and follow them in.

"Such the major hottie," Bec says the second the door shuts.

"How's it going?" Mel asks.

"Pretty good, I guess. We don't seem to have much to talk about. But I think it's just nervousness."

Becca puts an arm around my shoulder. "Don't worry. We'll be here for you."

I give her a stern look. "No, you won't. The deal was you could look, but now you've got to scram. I'm already too self-conscious."

They look disappointed. "Okay," Becca says. "But fill us in tomorrow."

After dinner, Alex and I walk out to the deck.

It's now-or-never time.

"Want to walk on the beach?" I ask him. "We can keep our distance from the water."

He smiles. "I'd love to."

From the deck, there's a boardwalk that goes out over the dunes. It's really amazing because at first you hear all the commotion of the restaurant, and the cars on the street. But, once you pass the dunes, all that sound is blocked out and all you hear are the wooden boards creaking beneath your feet and the surf washing up on the sand.

Luckily it's low tide, so there's a really wide stretch of sand for us to walk on.

"You should take off your shoes," I tell him. "The sand feels really good at night. There's water trapped under it and it keeps it cool."

He takes off his sneakers and tucks his socks in them. He goes to carry them.

I can't help but laugh.

"Just leave them," I say. "No one will take them."

He chuckles. "Okay. I guess that's the city boy in me."

I slip off my sandals and do the same.

"You're right," he says as we walk. "The sand does feel good at night."

This is everything I could hope for. The pauses in the conversation don't matter, because there are so many great sounds—the waves, the gulls, a nice breeze.

After a couple of blocks we come to a large wooden lifeguard chair. It's about twelve feet high to give the lifeguard a good view of the beach. And it's just wide enough for two people to cuddle in together.

We climb up and look out at the ocean. The moon is full and it's a cloudy night, so little shafts of light dance around us. Everything is great, except he obviously has something on his mind.

"I'm sorry if you didn't like Mama Taco's," I say.

"No," he answers. "I thought it was great."

I look over at him. "It's just that it seemed like something was bothering you a little. It still does."

He mulls this over. "Well, there is a problem, kind of."

Uh-oh, here's where I learn about the girl-friend back home in Washington.

"The problem is that I really like you," he says.

I smile. "And that's a problem?"

"In a way," he answers. "I don't live here. And, by the end of the summer, I'm going to have to go back home to Washington. So part of me says that it's not a good idea to get involved with anyone."

I think about it.

"Maybe," I say. "But I know that going in. What does that other part of you say?"

He pauses for a moment. "The other part says that I should just shut up and kiss you."

I smile. "I think that part's got it right."

We start to kiss lightly, and I can taste the salt air on his lips. Pretty soon, the kiss grows deeper and more passionate.

That's when I close my eyes, just like the girls in the movies.

Seventeen

It's the next morning and I'm still riding high from the date. I'm just munching away on my cereal and thinking about what a great time we had on the beach. Then my parents come into the room and start their daily comedy routine.

"Look at that," Mom says. "Janey's actually smiling at breakfast. That's unusual."

"That *is* unusual," Dad says. "Janey, why are you smiling?"

I roll my eyes. "Because I just love Honeycombs."

Dad nods. "That must be her pet name for him—Honeycombs."

I slap my spoon down. "I can't believe you just said that."

Mom leans over and gives me a kiss. "If you can't believe that, then you really haven't been paying attention for the last seventeen years. Did you have a good time last night?"

"Yes. End of story. New subject, please."

Dad raises his hands in frustration. "Come on. I had a whole routine worked out. I was just getting to my best stuff."

"Sorry," I say as I put my empty bowl in the sink. "You'll have to save it for Kendra."

Dad's not happy with this. "Kendra doesn't like my sense of humor," he mutters.

"Don't be ridiculous," Mom says, putting an arm around him. "Nobody likes your sense of humor."

Just then there's a knock at the door.

"That's for me," I say. "I've got to go to work."

"Wait one second," Dad says. "You don't start work this early." He turns to my mother. "She's trying to hoodwink us."

"*Hoodwink?* Dad, you so need to update your vocabulary. That's my ride because we have to drive all the way to Winter Park today. We're doing our little Beaver-Platypus dance and handing out Magic Waters flyers at the Winter Park Art Festival."

"Oh," he says. "In that case, drive safely."

I give him a kiss and head out the kitchen door. Winter Park is this great little city outside of Orlando. It's also more than two hours away. Grayson's volunteered to drive because he has an old Volvo station wagon big enough to hold our costumes.

"Good morning!" I say as I climb into Grayson's car.

"Ready to go to Winter Park?"

"I'm ready for all that overtime," I say with a smile.

He smiles too, and goes to start the car. But he hesitates for a moment.

"What's wrong?"

He looks at me. "When you start the car, the first song that you hear is crucial."

I can't believe my ears. Another freak like me. "You believe in Radio Karma too?"

He nods. "Absolutely. Although I've

never heard it called that. Can I use that term? Or do you have exclusive rights?"

"Feel free. Now, go ahead and start the car."

He gives me a nod and turns the key.

It's Ashlee Simpson, and she's screaming at the top of her lungs.

"You make me wanna La La
In the kitchen on the floor . . ."

He looks at me, and we both start to laugh. "See, this is obviously going to be a very intellectual journey."

"Obviously," I respond.

I can tell this is going to be a fun ride.

Just as we follow the highway out of Ruby Beach, he turns to me and smiles. "Tell me your most embarrassing moment?"

"What?"

"We've got two and a half hours to fill. So I thought we could start with embarrassing moments."

"I'd have to say that my most embarrassing moment is dressing up like a giant beaver every day."

"Well, *that's* understood. I'm talking about your next most embarrassing moment."

I don't know what to make of this guy. "You tell me yours first."

He thinks about it for a moment. "All right. I'll go first."

He takes a deep breath.

"Do you know what a bidet is? One of those fancy toilet things with the hose to wash your—"

"I know what it is," I cut him off.

"Well. I didn't. At least I didn't when I was ten. We were on vacation in New York City at this kind of ritzy hotel. Anyway, when we got to the room, I went into the bathroom and saw it there. And I just stared at it for a while trying to figure out what it might be."

"This is not going to end well, is it?"

"Finally, I did figure it out. Or at least I thought I did."

"You didn't!"

"Oh yes, I did. I called out, 'Mom, Dad, there's a water fountain in the bathroom.' They tried to rush in and stop me, but they were too late."

"Gross," I say, laughing and disgusted at the same time.

"Now you tell me yours."

"I don't want to be embarrassed."

"You're not going to be. You already know that I drank out of a bidet. It can't be worse than that."

"It's pretty close," I say.

I really don't want to do this, but for some reason I start to tell the story.

"This spring I took the SAT at the community college. About halfway through the test, I adjusted the way I was sitting and—"

He cuts me off. "Oh, my God. You're Fart Girl!"

"Fart Girl?" I say, mortified. "You mean, you heard about what happened?"

He starts laughing. "I didn't hear *about* it. I heard *it*. I was there, in the same classroom. I didn't know who did it, but I definitely heard it." He laughs some more. "The whole section was cracking up."

I am completely horrified. But, for some strange reason, I start to laugh. After all, if it had happened to anybody else, I'd think it was hilarious. And it *was* a serious tension breaker for everyone.

"Isn't it great?" he says.

"What?"

"We know each other's most embarrassing moments. That means we can talk
about absolutely anything. We've covered
the worst, so it can only go up from here."

I think about what he's saying and
smile. It makes sense. What happens next
is maybe the greatest conversation I've ever
had. We talk about anything and everything.

I confess that I also look at him a bit
differently now. I have ever since Melanie
pointed out how cute he was.

He tells me things about growing up
and what his school is like. And, unlike
most boys, he also seems genuinely interested in talking about me.

"Why do you swim the individual
medley?" he asks.

No one's ever asked me that before. It
takes me a moment to answer. "I think
because it takes all four strokes—breast,
back, butterfly, and free. So you can't just
specialize—you've got to be all around."

He looks at me for a moment. "That's a
good fit for you."

"What does that mean?"

"You're an all-around kind of girl, which is not easy to be in high school. School's geared to specializing—who's the best science student, who's the best debater, who's got the highest SATs—that kind of thing. I don't think the all-around people really get to shine until the reunion."

I don't think anyone has ever said anything nicer to me.

"Do you play any sports?" I ask.

He laughs. "I'm on the soccer team. Much to my dad's disappointment."

"Let me guess: He wanted a football player."

"Bingo. I may try out to be the kicker this year, just to make him happy. Although I know he doesn't think a kicker is really a football player."

We talk about the party at Michelle's house, and he asks about Becca and Melanie.

"Becca's a funny one," I tell him. "I don't know if you noticed, but she's really pretty."

I look over at him, and he tries not to

react too much. "Yeah, I noticed," he says with a laugh.

"I think it makes her self-conscious. Too many guys just hit on her, so she kind of shuts them all out. She's really withdrawn, which a lot of people take to mean that she's a bitch. But she isn't at all.

"Melanie's the quietest one of the group," I continue. "She's just really shy."

"Why?"

"I don't know. She always kind of was. But it got worse freshman year when her mom died."

He looks over at me while we drive along the highway. "Did her mother have cancer?"

I'm stunned. "How did you know that?"

"I noticed she was wearing a Live Strong bracelet."

Despite Becca's belief that you can count on guys not to notice little things, he picked that out in a party in the dark with a girl he'd never met.

"She had breast cancer," I tell him. "She was really great, Mrs. White. She was like my second mother. Her funeral was the saddest thing I've ever seen. Becca and I were bawling our eyes out, but Melanie didn't cry one bit.

"Pretty soon, I stopped listening to all of the things that people were saying about her mother and I just watched Melanie sit there stone-faced. I couldn't believe it. Her expression never changed. It took me a year just to ask her about it."

"What did she say?"

"She told me she was worried that if she started crying, she might never stop. I think her way of coping is becoming a doctor. She spent so much time at the hospital that last year."

"Does she ever talk about it?"

"Nope. She loves to talk about her mom. But she never says anything about that year or the cancer."

"She's lucky she has you two as friends."

"Thanks." Just then I look up and realize that we're already in Winter Park. I've lost all track of time. Just like the other night when I swam past midnight.

I guess that's what happens when you're comfortable.

We have a great time at the art festival and another incredible conversation on the way home. It's funny, because any other year, I'd be head over heels for Grayson. He's just the type of guy I always wanted to find. I can't help but wonder what might have happened if I hadn't met Alex.

Eighteen

"Why are we stopping at the YMCA?" Alex asks a bit nervously as we pull into the parking lot.

"We're here for your next lesson," I explain. "Swimming in public."

He chuckles a little bit and then stops cold. "I don't really think that's a good idea."

"Of course you don't," I say. "Because, so far, you've only been able to swim *with* me and *in* your backyard."

He considers this and nods. "And I'm okay with that."

"Well, I'm not. You need to get over all your fears. I can't be your permanent life preserver, and if the only place you can swim is in your dad's pool, then all of this will have been for nothing."

We head to the entrance, and he stops cold. "But when we first agreed to all this, you *promised* that you'd keep it a secret. How are you going to do that if you're giving me a lesson in front of everyone?"

"Easy," I tell him. "I'm not going to give you any instruction. We're just going to act like we're here having fun."

He frowns. "Not really my idea of a hot date."

"Get over it."

The pool deck is completely packed with kids, which is exactly what I wanted. It's loud and noisy and seems totally uncontrolled. If he can swim here, he'll do fine anywhere.

First we lay our towels down on a pair of lounge chairs. I take off my shorts and shirt to reveal a sporty new one-piece I bought at Hixon's Surf Shop. (No way am I wearing a bikini at the Y. I just know too many people here.)

"Let me help you with that," he says as I put on some sunscreen. I give him a sly smile, and he squirts some on my back. He rubs it in, and it's almost more than I can take. The thing is, he's completely not trying to be sexy about it. But it totally is.

"Enough stalling," I say. "Let's get in the water."

We hold hands as we go over to the shallow end. To anybody watching, it just seems like we're girlfriend and boyfriend. (Which we kind of are.) But this way I can help him feel safe without anyone knowing.

"This is okay," he says as we slide into the waist-deep water.

I pull him close and whisper into his ear, "Now I want you to try the back float."

He gives me a pained look.

"Trust me," I say. "I won't let anything bad happen."

He takes a deep breath. "Okay."

I've got my arms around him, but it still just looks like we're a couple. He leans back, and I slowly lower him down until he's floating.

"See, no one suspects a thing."

Floating in a pool by yourself is one thing. Doing it surrounded by a dozen kids playing Marco Polo is something else. There's a lot of splashing, yelling, and bumping. But, amazingly, he does fine through all of it.

After a couple of minutes, I tell him that he can stand up. "You're doing super."

When he gets up, he shoots an evil eye at this one kid who splashed him a bunch. But he's obviously happy with his progress.

"Just one more thing," I say.

I can tell by his look that he's not looking forward to this. "What?"

"Five seconds . . . underwater."

"You really hate me, don't you?"

"Now, you know that's not true," I say with a wink. "Don't worry—I'll go under with you."

He concentrates for a moment and nods. Then he takes one big breath and goes underwater. I go right with him and count off the time with my fingers. When I reach five, he still stays under. This makes me smile, and a stream of bubbles escapes from my mouth. I keep counting off on my fingers until I reach ten and we both go back to the surface.

"Show-off," I say.

"So? Did I pass?" he asks.

I nod. "Absolutely."

"Good. Now I want you to do something for me."

"Like what?" I ask suspiciously.

He motions over to where three lanes are marked off for lap swimming. "I want to see you swim."

"What are you talking about? You see me swim all the time."

"You're not really swimming. You're demonstrating strokes or showing me how to float. I want to see you swim *fast*."

"No way."

"Why not?"

"'Cause I'd feel stupid."

"You're talking to a guy who just got intimidated by a five-year-old playing Marco Polo."

I really can't believe this. But it's also kind of sweet. "Okay, I'll do it," I say without a shred of conviction.

He takes a seat in the bleachers, and I dive into the last lane. I really can't believe I'm doing this. I lean my head back in the water to slick my hair back.

He flashes a big cheesy grin and gives me

a signal to get started. I have been swimming for as long as I can remember. But in all that time, I've never felt so self-conscious.

I do an easy lap down and back.

"Happy?" I ask, looking out from the water.

He comes over to be close (but not too close) and narrows his eyes. "I thought you said you were fast."

He's tapped into my competitive side. I realize he's not going to stop until I show him what I can do.

"Okay, float boy," I joke. "Sit down and watch."

I swim another lap, but, unlike the first one, I put a little effort into it. I do another and another. Each lap is faster than the last. The more I swim, the less self-conscious I feel. Over the final twenty-five yards I do a full-out sprint that leaves me gasping for air. When I catch my breath, I look up and see him in the bleachers.

"Wow," he says with a smile. "Watch out, USC."

Suddenly, I feel self-conscious again, but in a good way. I climb out of the water and towel off.

"You weren't lying," he said. "You really are fast. That's cool."

While I'm basking in my moment, I decide to take a chance. "Speaking of cool," I say, "how would you like to go to a cool party tonight?"

"Sounds interesting. What kind of party?"

"It's a big Tragic Waters employee party, down on the beach."

He nods. "That sounds great."

"Why don't you pick me up at Magic Waters after you get off work? Then we can go over there together."

"This isn't some elaborate plot to get me into Magic Waters, is it?"

"Absolutely not," I assure him. "You can meet me in the parking lot. The very dry parking lot."

He flashes that gorgeous smile, and I try to remind myself that he won't be around for long. I try to tell myself not to fall in love. But it's really way too late for that.

Nineteen

It's ninety-five degrees. That's outside. Climb inside forty pounds of shag carpet beaver costume and you begin to understand why I get a little light-headed sometimes.

Today, though, it's had no effect on me. Just the thought of going to the party with Alex tonight has put me in a great mood all day long. (I'm in such a good mood that I even smiled at Crystal in the lunchroom.)

Our "meet and greet" shows have never been better. They've been high energy, and the crowds have really responded. Now all I have to do is dance in the parade and I'll be done.

The parade starts at the main entrance to the park. All of the characters gather around the pirate ship turned birthday cake and dance to a dreadful song called "It's Been a Nifty Fifty Years." Just a taste of it so you can understand my struggle:

> *"Get your sons, get your daughters,*
> *Head right down to Magic Waters.*
> *For fifty years it's been fun*
> *To splash around in the sun.*
> *Now come along and dance with me.*
> *It's our Golden Jamboree . . ."*

At this point, the marching band plays and all of the characters are supposed to run into the crowd and pick a guest as a dance partner. (Think it's tough getting a guy to dance with you at a party, try asking him when you're dressed like a deranged woodland creature.)

I always go for balding, middle-aged men. Though not normally my type, they're usually dads and more than willing to play along.

Today I find the perfect guy. He's there with his wife and kids and he's wearing a

shirt that says F.B.I. FEMALE BODY INSPECTOR.
If he's not too embarrassed to wear that, he
shouldn't be too embarrassed to dance with
a giant beaver.

We dance for a little bit, and his kids
totally eat it up. When the song ends, we
signal for everyone to follow us as we begin
our march through the park toward the
mermaid lagoon.

That's when I see him.

It's hard to see through the eye slits, so
I look back to be sure. Suddenly I feel
woozy—and it's not because of the heat.

Right there, in the middle of the parade
crowd—it's Alex.

Instead of meeting after work, he's
come early to surprise me. Even though
he's totally terrified of water, he's walking
through a giant water theme park to see
me. And it would be the sweetest thing in
the world, if only I weren't lying to him at
the moment.

This parade is heading directly to the
mermaid lagoon. The same mermaid
lagoon where he thinks I currently am a
mermaid. When we get there and he sees
the girls in the water, Bikini Jane will

become Why Did You Lie to Me Jane in the blink of an eye.

I start to hyperventilate, which is not a good idea in an overheated, confined space.

In my growing hysteria, I realize that I have two things working in my favor. The first is the fact that the parade blocks off the entire park. There's no way for him to get to the lagoon ahead of us. He's got to march in the parade, where I can keep an eye on him.

My second positive is that my costume completely obscures my real identity. I can get right up to him and he won't know it's me.

I consider taking him out with my tail. After all, it worked on those two guys in the band and I can make it look like an accident. But I can't risk actually hurting him. Instead, I just kind of dance around him and act like it's part of the show.

I have hit rock bottom.

I have become: Stalker Beaver Chick.

From the entrance, we march through Dolphin Cove—the part of the park dedicated to "Education and Conservation." It's hard to take the claim seriously when you consider it features a dolphin show called If Fish Could Wish. (This totally overlooks the fact that dolphins are mammals and not fish.)

The two stars of the show are the beloved park mascots Bubbles and Beauregard. At least, those are their stage names. The original Bubbles and Beauregard died decades ago and have been portrayed by countless dolphins since. The current two are actually named Hector and Frank.

As I continue my stalking, I notice that Alex is unnerved walking past the dolphin tank. I begin to hope that his fear of water will freak him out so much that he'll have to turn back before we reach the mermaid lagoon. (Am I evil or what?)

I even stall him right next to the tank until Hector—as he's been trained to do— swims by and splashes the crowd. Alex recoils when he's hit by the water, and I am wracked with guilt.

We are almost to the mermaid lagoon when I get an idea. It's pure desperation, but it's the best that I can come up with.

I grab Alex by the hand and start dancing with him. I'm counting on the fact that he's too polite to say no. (This is classic—our one and only dance will be with me as Eager Beaver.)

After a few moves I lead him over to the birthday cake float. Luckily, he doesn't break free of my grip. I take him to the parade supervisor, who's walking directly behind the float, and I break Eager Beaver Rule number one: I talk in costume.

All I say is, "King Neptune."

The supervisor looks at Alex and nods in agreement. She takes over from there, and I breathe a sigh of relief.

At the end of the parade a guest is picked from the crowd and crowned King Neptune. He gets a trident and a crown and stands on top of the birthday cake float when the firework goes off.

Normally the supervisor picks the guest, but I was counting on Alex's dreamy eyes to win her over and they did perfectly.

I watch in great relief as Alex is led behind the scenes for a quick costume change. By the time he gets back and climbs to the top of the cake, the mermaids have already dived underwater and out of sight.

In a weird way, I'm thrilled with the brilliance of my plan. But I'm also troubled by it. When I first lied about the mermaid thing, it was a sudden reaction. But this was cold and calculated.

I don't really have time to worry about it, though. As soon as the parade is over, I rush back to the warehouse and ditch my costume. I jump in the shower so that it looks like I've been swimming and then I head straight for the employee exit.

I'm relieved when I see Alex standing there with a smile on his face. (At least that means I got away with my plan.) He's talking to someone I can't make out. But when he moves out of the way, I see who it is and my heart sinks.

He's talking to Crystal.

If I was panicked during the parade, I'm mortified now. Nothing good can come out of Alex talking with Crystal. I brace myself and smile. I decide to act like everything's just peachy.

"Hey, Alex."

"Hi, Jane."

I wait for what seems forever, and it's apparent that Crystal's not going anywhere.

"I see you've met Crystal."

Crystal flashes her phony smile. "I was just telling Alex that you and I go way back—all the way to elementary school."

I can't believe she's acting like we're friends. "Way back. Fourth grade, I think."

The three of us talk for a moment, and it turns out that Crystal just struck up a conversation when she saw a hot guy standing there. (Apparently that's what these girls just do.)

It's all mindless and excruciating. Then Alex mentions that he just got off work at the country club.

"You work at Lake Shelby?" she asks ever so sweetly, her accent blooming like a magnolia tree. "My family's got a membership there."

I can't believe he's so oblivious to the fact that she's a total phony. If I weren't currently involved in a major deception myself, I'd be offended.

"Well, if you ever need a tennis lesson," he says, "I'll be there."

No! He can't give her a tennis lesson. He's supposed to give me one. Tell me that there isn't a conspiracy against me.

That's all the invitation that Crystal needs. "I might just take you up on that." She turns on her smile, heaves her breasts, and actually says, "Toodles."

And on the eighth day God created evil and he named it Crystal Gentry.

What's done is done. At least Alex doesn't seem to have noticed that I'm not a mermaid.

Once we're alone, he reaches over and gives me a kiss, which is pretty cool.

"You wouldn't believe it. There was a guy in the park today who looked just like you," I say. "He was crowned King Neptune."

"That *was* me." He hands me the ceremonial photograph they gave him. "I came early to see you and I got swept up in the parade."

"Didn't you say you'd never come here?" (I was kind of counting on that being true.)

"I know, but I got off work early and I thought I'd surprise you."

"Surprise is the word for it."

We're almost to the car when I take another hit. Grayson is running after us.

"Jane! Jane!"

When he reaches us, he's smiling huge.

"I'm sorry to chase you down like that, but I just wanted to say that you were great today. Really terrific in every show."

A warning starts playing in my head. *Danger. Danger.*

"I can't believe I missed it," Alex says.

The warning speeds up. *Danger. Danger. Danger.*

Grayson turns to him and smiles. They shake hands, and it kind of freaks me out. After all, one is sort of my boyfriend and the other is sort of—well, I don't know what to call him, but it's weird to see them together.

"You must be Alex. My name's Grayson. I work in the show with Jane."

"I didn't know they had male mermaids too."

The warning stops. It's too late. I'm dead. At first, Grayson is confused, but he puts it all together pretty quickly. His smile fades, and he nods.

"Well, I'm not actually in the show," he says weakly. "I work on the technical crew."

Alex is oblivious. "So will you be at the party tonight?"

Grayson nods. "Yeah. I'll be there."

"Great. Maybe we'll see you."

"Yeah, maybe."

Through this entire encounter I'm speechless. I am now Mute Jane.

Grayson's nothing but a great and decent guy. Not only has he discovered that I'm not so great and decent, but I've dragged him into it with me. The look he gives me as he walks away stings. It's not anger. It's not even frustration.

It's the look of total disappointment.

Twenty

About forty-five of my fellow employees are enrolled in the Magic Waters College Program. They're all students from colleges and universities across the country. They get actual school credit for spending a semester working at the park and taking a couple classes at the community college.

I don't really understand the academic value of selling rain ponchos, but I can't blame someone who's freezing to death at Youngstown State for wanting to spend a few months in warm, sunny Florida.

All the kids in the program are housed in a little trailer park just outside of town. The sign at the trailer park's entrance features a picture of none other than yours truly—Eager Beaver—which is why everyone calls it Beaver Town.

By the time we get there, the parking lot is overflowing with cars. We end up parking about a quarter mile away and walking up along the beach. As we get close, I try to warn Alex about what's ahead.

"This is called a jukebox party," I tell him. "They have it twice a year and it's a really big deal."

"What's a jukebox party?"

"There are fifteen trailers at the park, each with three roommates. Last week they had a drawing and each trailer was assigned a particular type of music. The roommates have had a week to decorate according to their type of music."

"Sounds like fun!"

"It is. But it can also be a little wild."

Just as we're about to reach the trailer park, I stop.

"There's one thing I have to say before we go in there."

"What's that?"

"We've never really talked about it, so I don't know if you drink or not. But if you want to tonight, that's cool. I just want to drive home, ya know? See, a big part of my dad's job is going to accident scenes and, well, I just won't ride with someone even if they've only had one beer—"

He cuts me off with a wave of his hand. "Don't worry about it," he says. "That's totally cool. I'll just have soda."

Our first stop is at Trailer #8, which is reggae themed. The three girls who live here are all wearing fake dreadlock wigs and Bob Marley shirts. One of them is Denise, a girl from California who plays Ollie Otter.

I introduce her to Alex.

"Hey, mon," she says with an over-the-top accent. "Welcome to Jamaica. We got a beach in there." She motions to her trailer.

"A beach?"

"Check it out."

We walk in and, sure enough, there's a beach. Or rather an inflatable kiddie pool and about ten pounds of sand spread all over the floor. It'll be a bitch to clean up, but it's pretty funny.

"I feel like I'm actually in Jamaica," Alex says with a laugh.

"Ya, mon," I say, getting into the vibe. "Me too."

We dance in Jamaica for a little while and then we start going from trailer to trailer. I really like the disco-themed trailer with the mirrored ball hanging from the ceiling, but I could live without the heavy metal one.

My favorite, though, is the polka trailer. It sounds totally ridiculous, but that's what makes it fun. The three guys who live there are wearing lederhosen and they're playing it absolutely straight-faced. Every half hour they lead a group in the chicken dance and it is beyond hilarious.

Right outside the polka trailer we run into Grayson.

"Grayson, are you having fun?" I ask, hoping that he's forgotten about the episode in the parking lot.

He nods. "Totally. But, I'm warning you, stay away from Trailer Fourteen."

"What music is it?" Alex asks.

"Gregorian chants," Grayson says with a raised eyebrow. "And the weird thing is, some kids are hanging out there."

"Thanks for the warning," I say.

"Does anyone know where I can find a rest room?" Alex asks.

"Right by the pool," Grayson says, pointing the way.

Alex turns to me. "Can you wait here for a second?"

I nod, and Alex hurries over to the rest room, leaving Grayson and me alone for a moment.

"Listen," I say. "I want to explain about what happened in the parking lot. The whole mermaid thing."

"You don't have to explain anything," Grayson answers.

"You don't understand."

He takes a breath. "I understand completely. You know, at first I couldn't figure out why you were the one picking King Neptune out of the crowd. But I figured it out on the way over here. That was the only way to keep him from seeing the mermaids. Clever."

I can't believe he saw that, too.

"He must be some great guy for you to go to all that trouble."

"He really is," I tell him. "Why don't

you go around with us for a while? You can get to know him."

He's quiet for a moment, and I can't really read his reaction. "That'd be cool. But I think we're headed in different directions."

He smiles and disappears into the polka trailer.

A few minutes later, my life slips completely into conspiracy mode when Alex and I run into Crystal.

She beams upon seeing him and goes into instant predator mode.

"It's Alex, right?" she coos with the slur of a few too many beers.

"That's right."

"Are you and Jane having fun tonight?"

It's amazing how she can mention me and totally ignore me all at the same time.

"Nothing but," Alex says.

She slides up and leans right into him—partly as a come-on, partly to keep her balance. "I'm heading over to Trailer Four for a little hula dancing. You should stop by."

"We'll make sure to do that," I say,

redirecting the conversation and Alex. "Right now, we're just going to relax over by the pool."

"Typical Jane," she says, finally acknowledging me. "She can't get enough of those pools."

She staggers off to Hulaville while Alex and I head over toward the pool and kick back on a couple of beach chairs.

"So what do you think of the jukebox party?" I ask.

"It's cool," he says. "I never would have known such a thing existed."

We sit and chat for a little while. It's really great, until all hell breaks loose. It starts when the three guys from the heavy metal trailer come and sit nearby.

Apparently we weren't the only ones to make a quick exit. Their trailer is completely empty, and they're pissed and totally wasted.

"Want a beer?" one of them says, offering a bottle to Alex.

"No thanks," he answers.

The guy looks at him like he's speaking Swahili and tries to get up in Alex's face. "Dude, c'mon."

Alex rolls his eyes at me, and we get up to go.

Then I hear it. It's the kind of thing that sounds funny to someone who's drunk, but totally not so much to the sober among us.

"Let's throw him in the pool."

All the color drains from Alex's face.

I try to stop it, but I can't. Two of them grab him by the arms and legs and head toward the pool. The water is dark and deep, and there's no way he can do this. Alex panics and he starts trying to kick his way free.

"What is wrong with you?" one of the guys says. "We're just trying to have some fun."

Alex tries to say something, but he can't. He's breathing way too hard, and his face is bright red. I start yelling, but they ignore me.

Just as they are about to throw him in the water, the cavalry arrives. And it's none other than Grayson.

"Wait, wait," he says. "Aren't you guys from the heavy metal trailer?"

"Yeah."

"Do you know who Bethany Buck and Julie Komorn are?"

"Should we?"

"They're only the hottest girls in the mermaid show. And right now, they're at your trailer and they are so wasted."

They drop Alex without a word and run right for their trailer.

Alex takes a moment to catch his breath and manages to sputter out a thank-you to Grayson.

Grayson sort of shrugs. "We should probably get out of here. Once those guys get to their trailer and realize it's empty, they'll come after both of us."

Alex nods. "Good call."

We hurry through Beaver Town and make our way down to the beach. Only there, after he's had a few moments to stop and let the adrenaline die down, does Alex really say anything. I stand there and watch as the two of them bond over the moment.

"I really want to thank you," Alex says, still breathing heavily. "I'm kind of frightened to death of water."

Grayson laughs. "Good thing we ran to the ocean."

Finally Alex laughs a little. "Good thing we're all pretty fast."

"I was particularly impressed with the way you jumped over that chain-link fence."

As the three of us walk down the beach and toward Alex's car, I'm stunned by the chain of events. Two boys, both nice and fairly attractive, now bonded over some weird encounter with drunk metal heads threatening bodily harm. And it wouldn't have happened if they hadn't met me first.

I think the conspiracy to ruin my life is beginning to endanger innocent bystanders.

Twenty-one

After weeks of preparation, Alex is ready for his final lesson. It's time for him to take his Pollywog swim test.

When I knock on the door, I brace myself for the chance that Josie's going to answer.

"You're lucky," he says as he opens the door. "It's just me."

"Hallelujah."

Alex seems way excited. In the kitchen, he picks up a camcorder.

"What's that for?" I ask.

He looks a little embarrassed. "I want you to tape me in the water. So I can send it to my mom. It's been ten years and I want her to stop worrying."

One time I read a magazine article that said the way a boy treats his mother is the same way he'll treat a girlfriend. I don't know if it's true, but if so, this is just another reason to say, "Sign me up."

When we get to the pool, he turns on the camera. He narrates as he pans across the pool. "Hi, Mom. This is Dad's ridiculously large pool, spa, waterfall."

He continues panning and stops at me. "And this is Jane, whom I already told you about. A state champion swimmer and licensed CPR instructor. So don't worry. Say hello, Jane."

I wave into the camera. "Hello, Alex's mom."

(Don't think I missed the part about him already telling his mother about me. Forget floating in water—I could float on air.)

He puts the camera down on a table and walks to the edge of the pool.

"Are you ready?" I ask him.

He takes a deep breath. "Absolutely. I even got new trunks."

I laugh. "Trunks?"

He points to his bathing suit. "Aren't these called trunks?"

"By our grandparents, maybe," I say, giving him a hard time. "Those are board shorts."

He tries it out. "Board shorts. Yeah, better."

"Let's see how they do in the water, Pollywog."

He gives me a defiant look. "That's Mr. Pollywog to you."

With that, he sheds his shirt (giving me one more reason to live) and dives into the water. Okay, "dive" is not the right word, but he starts off on the pool deck and ends up in the pool—so we'll call it a dive.

I get out my clipboard and checklist.

"Aren't you coming in?"

"Only in case of an emergency," I explain. "This is your test." (It also means my hair scrunch might last, for a change.)

I run him through all the requirements: twenty-five yards on his stomach, twenty-fiv yards on his back, tread water for sixty seconds. Every now and then I grab the camera and shoot him in action. None of it is pretty, but all of it is swimming. He's beaming with joy.

It gets down to the last skill.

"I want you to swim the length of the pool underwater," I tell him.

"Underwater?" He sounds a little panicked, but I know he can do it.

"Trust me. Strike that. Trust yourself. You can do it."

He nods.

I hope this is the right thing to do. Technically, he's already completed what he needs for Pollywog, but I want him to build his confidence some more.

He takes a deep breath and goes underwater. For the next thirty seconds he's not a hunk or a stud. He's just a student and I'm his teacher. I videotape the whole thing for his mother.

My mom's told me about students who struggle in her English class only to blossom in the end. She says it's the reason she keeps teaching, and I can understand why.

The last ten yards are shaky, and I wonder if I'll have to jump in. But he keeps going and when he gets there, he bursts through the surface with a goofy grin on his face.

"I did it," he pants before sucking air. "I did it."

I'm beyond excited and, before I know it, I put down the camera and jump right into the water with him despite the fact that I'm still wearing clothes over my swimsuit.

"You did it! You swam the whole thing."

I throw my arms around him.

He smiles and—for the first time since I've met him—he's relaxed in the water.

"Wow!" he says. "I can't believe it. You're a really good teacher."

He stops for a second and looks at me. "I thought you said you would only come in the water for an emergency."

Suddenly, I'm quite aware of the fact that I jumped in like a madwoman.

What would Bikini Jane do?

"It *is* an emergency. I realized that you needed to kiss someone."

I wipe my hair out of my eyes and smile.

We lean in to kiss, but he stops before our lips touch. "Wait a second," he says. "Where's my certificate?"

"What certificate?"

"On the first day you said I'd get a

Pollywog certificate. You even took my picture for it."

You mean the shot of you and your bare-chested glory that I took so I could show you off to my girlfriends.

"That certificate. Sure. I can only order it after you've completed the program. It's all very official."

Note to self: I will need to design an official-looking Pollywog certificate on my computer tonight.

He goes to kiss me and once again stops short. He's playing with me, but I can take it.

"After work, will you come by the club so I can give you your first tennis lesson?"

"Yes," I say. "Now, will you stop talking?"

We lean in and kiss. It's a long, wonderful kiss right there in the deep end of the pool.

Chlorine never tasted so good.

Twenty-two

The Lake Shelby Country Club is the most exclusive in the area. It's beautiful and all, but I've never really had much use for it. I'm more of a hang out at the beach, swim at the Y kind of girl. In my entire life, I've only been to the club twice before—once for a birthday party, and again for a junior swim meet.

Today I've come for my tennis lesson with Alex. I check in at the pro shop.

"I'm looking for Alex Walker."

The man behind the counter smiles and points toward the courts. "He's giving a lesson right now. It should be over soon; if you want to walk out there you can wait."

There are four tennis courts grouped together. I can see Alex at the far one. He calls out to his student: "Nice and steady ground strokes. Perfect."

It's cool to see him in his element. In the pool he was all scared, but here he's clearly at ease. It's nice. At least, it is until I see his student. My heart sinks—again. Crystal Gentry is making her move.

I take a seat in the little grandstands and wave. He waves back and says that they're almost done.

Crystal just ignores me.

The rest of the lesson is total agony. I have to watch a guy I'm crazy about play tennis with my nemesis, who, oh by the way, happens to have a scorching-hot body.

She uses it like a weapon. At one point she bends over to pick up a ball and her little skirt flips up so that she shows off her butt. (Which I'd kill for.) Later, she reaches down to pick up a ball at the net and she gives him the ultimate cleavage shot. (They may be store-bought, but they're well done.) Alex can't help but look. He is after all a guy.

I want to stand up and shout, "Everybody knows they're fake."

She does it so well that part of me has to marvel at it. She's evil genius personified. It doesn't take long to realize that this show isn't just for him. It's for me, too. She wants me to know what I'm up against. She's trying to intimidate me straight out of the competition.

It's not going to work.

When the lesson finally ends, she looks up and acts like she's just seen me for the first time.

"Hey there, Jane." She says it like we're old friends. Which, actually, we once were.

"Hey, guys. How was the lesson?"

I was talking to Alex, but she decides to answer first. "Incredible. Our guy is really something." As she says this, she puts her hand on his shoulder.

Our guy? She's the one who's really something. I've got to fight back. I've got to do something. That's when I think of it. I've got to make her look bad. But how?

"I don't suppose you've got enough energy left to play a set."

Her face transforms, and she gives me

that "killer cheerleader from hell" look. You don't get to be the queen bee of a large high school without having a serious competitive streak.

"I'm a little winded," she says ever so sweetly. "But that sounds like fun."

Poor Alex. He's oblivious. (Guys are so that way.) He really thinks we're two close friends about to have a fun round of tennis. But this is where the war will be fought. And the best thing is that I'm actually pretty good at tennis. Melanie and I played all last summer.

"I'll serve," Crystal says as she heads to the baseline. As she gets in position, the still oblivious Alex shouts out some encouraging instruction.

"Remember to throw the ball straight up and arch your back."

Crystal smiles like she had no idea what to do. Then she morphs into Serena Williams and rockets a serve right past my head. It's a warning shot. The damsel in tennis distress we saw during the lesson bears no resemblance to this girl, who has obviously spent much of her life at the country club.

What follows is an epic battle. Crystal has better ball control, but I've got more endurance. She kills me with shots in the corners, and I try to run her ragged from side to side. I'm counting on the fact that she's got a body made for mermaiding, not for running around.

During one point I'm all over the court, returning everything she's got. Finally, she leaves an opening and I crush the ball right past her and, in a rather unladylike way, she falls to the ground.

As she brushes herself off, she drops her first bomb. "My, oh my," she says in that sweet Southern accent. "Aren't you a busy little *beaver*?"

She stresses the last word to make sure that I've gotten the message.

Two points later she goes down again. This time, faking an ankle sprain.

Alex rushes over to help her off the court.

"I'll be fine," she says as she throws her arm around him and he helps her from the court. This gives her the perfect opportunity to press her chest against him.

"I guess we'll have to call this one a

draw," she says, knowing full well that she's already won.

Alex is completely falling for her injured act. He helps her to a bench and then starts feeling her ankle. This of course puts him right in front of her with her short little skirt and her perfect long legs. Now she moves in for the kill.

"I was talking to Alex about Fourth of July and he said you two are going to the fireworks together."

Okay, where is this going?

"Yeah?"

"Well, my boyfriend's going to be out of town. I was wondering if I could hang out with you guys. I don't want to be a third wheel, but if it's not a problem . . ."

This is unbelievable. She's trying to squirrel in on my date. She's making a move. (He, by the way, is still oblivious and feeling up her ankle.) I'm about to put my foot down. To tell her hell no. Then she drops her second, far more deadly bomb. Who knows how long she's been holding it, but she's chosen her moment.

"After all, we mermaids have to stick together."

I almost fall back. She knows about the lie. She knows he thinks I'm a mermaid. And she's let me know she'll spill the beans if I don't go along with her.

"I'd love for you to come."

Twenty-three

"We are taking that bitch down."

You gotta love Becca. I've just told her and Mel about my little tennis match with Crystal, and she's ready for war.

Melanie shakes her head in amazement. "I can't believe she put the moves on a guy *while you were with him*! That's low even for her."

"And now she's going on *your* date to see the fireworks."

"It gets worse," I tell them.

"How could it be worse?"

"I just got a call from work. It turns out that Eager Beaver is going to be part of the Fourth of July celebration. We've got to do our dance and pose for pictures with kids."

"Does that mean . . . ?" Melanie asks.

"Yes. That means I will have to leave my crush of crushes with Crystal Gentry while I sneak away and dress up like a huge beaver."

Becca's getting mad. "I bet she knew. I bet she already knew when she weaseled into your date."

I lie back on my bed and stare at the ceiling. I can't believe this is happening. "I should have known better than to go after a guy like that. He's out of my league."

"Don't say that," Becca complains. "You didn't go after him. You *got* him. And, if you're not in his league, it's because you own his league. The problem is Crystal."

Melanie paces around the room for a minute, trying to come up with a solution. "Somehow you need to be Eager Beaver and Bikini Jane at the same time."

Melanie looks at the picture of Janus on the sign above my bed. "You've got to be like Janus—one you, two faces."

Suddenly, I have an idea. I don't know if it's pure brilliance or just desperate. But it comes to me and I start to get excited. So excited that I reach across the bed and poke Becca's tattoo.

"Buzz, buzz, buzz!"

"What? What?" Becca asks. "You figured it out?"

"I could be in two places at once . . . if someone else was in the beaver costume."

This sinks in for a moment.

"That's hot," Becca says. "That'll work."

I smile and look right at her. "Good. 'Cause you have to be the other person."

Suddenly, the smile disappears from her face.

"Whoa, whoa, whoa. Why does it have to be me?"

"It can't be Mel. She's only five feet two. The costume won't fit her."

Becca's still not getting on board. "But, isn't Eager Beaver kind of all cheerful and cuddly? Those aren't words that go real well with me."

"No, but they could be. Think about it. If you can teach me to walk like Jennifer Garner, don't you think I can teach you to hop around like Eager Beaver?"

She is totally not buying this.

"Would you do it . . . for me?"

I give her the same look I used on my dad when I was trying to talk him into getting me a car.

"Hell, no. Does that face work on Alex? Because it sure doesn't work on me."

Melanie chimes in. "Screw that. Would you do it to piss off Crystal?"

That seals it.

Becca smiles. "Yeah, that works. I'd do it for that."

On the night of July 3, Becca and Melanie come over to my house for a makeover much different from the one that produced Bikini Jane.

Tonight we're creating Becca the Beaver.

She's a little bit taller and a whole lot curvier than I am, so the fur bodysuit is really snug. She instantly discovers what Mrs. Claus warned me about at orientation: The costume tends to bind in the bust.

She lets loose with a flurry of Spanish words that I assume are not family-friendly. When she's done, she gives me her meanest look.

"You will owe me for the rest of your life."

"I know. I know. But we can worry about that later. Now, let's see you walk."

Melanie and I watch as Becca saunters across the room and back. We're both stunned.

"What? Is something wrong?" Becca asks.

"Yes, something's wrong," I say, dumbfounded. "That was sexy. How the hell can you look sexy wearing a giant beaver costume?"

Becca can't help but smile. "You can put a cover over a Ferrari, but the engine's still going to purr."

Mel and I both laugh. Only Becca could get away with a line like that.

"Let's try to keep it under the speed limit."

Next we adjust the beaver head to Becca's head so that she can see out of the eye slits. It takes a little getting used to, and she runs smack into the door.

When she finally gets the hang of it (sort of), I spend an hour going over the rules and practicing the dance Eager

Beaver does with Platypus Rex and Ollie Otter.

Becca has a little trouble with the rules. (Especially the one that says she can't slug a kid who pulls her tail.) But she gets them all down. The dance is a different story. Grayson and I have practiced it together all summer. It's too difficult to master in one night.

We decide on an alternate plan. Becca will do the first forty-five minutes of shaking hands and posing for pictures, and then we'll sneak off somewhere and switch places before the dance. While I'm away, Melanie will run interference between Crystal and Alex.

It's not much of a plan, but it's all we've got.

Operation Busy Beaver is all set.

Twenty-four

The next day I work a normal shift at Tragic Waters and rush home to get ready. It's beyond awkward (and a little bit surreal) to see my date pick me up with my arch nemesis riding in the passenger seat. (They live near each other, so he picked her up first.)

Crystal has taken this one step further by asking if she can stay in the front seat when we drive to see the fireworks. She says she needs the room for the ankle she sprained during our tennis match. She even has it wrapped in a bandage, which is funny because it wasn't wrapped at work today.

I go along with it. I've got a lot riding

today and I need all the good karma I can get.

The Fourth of July is a big deal in Ruby Beach. There's always a huge town party down at Russell Park. My dad and the rest of his crew give free rides in the fire truck. The high school band plays patriotic songs. And there are tables covered with free watermelon.

The highlight of the evening is the fireworks display shot off from the end of the pier over the ocean. Unlike the "display" at Tragic Waters, this one is really something special.

Crystal is putting on quite a display herself as she hobbles her way to a bench. The three of us sit there and make painfully dull small talk. I can tell that Crystal is waiting for me to leave so that I can become Eager Beaver. And the longer I go without leaving, the more it drives her crazy.

She almost dies when the Magic Waters characters come out and start mingling with the crowd. They're all there: Platypus Rex, Ollie Otter, and—miraculously—Eager Beaver.

Crystal gives me a look, and I smile.

Becca obviously sees us, because she

makes a point to walk right up to us. She bends down and dramatically rubs Crystal's sore ankle. She even bends over and gives her a hug. (It's almost more than I can take.) For the first time ever, Eager Beaver's huge, gap-toothed smile seems appropriate.

"Hey there, Eager Beaver," I say.

Becca turns to me and gives me a big thumbs-up. Inside, I'm sure she's flipping me off, but she's going along with it, and that's why I love her.

Becca isn't exactly graceful in the costume. She trips over a kid and slams into a phone booth. But, in a weird way, she seems to be enjoying it.

She dances with a group of kids, playfully steals someone's watermelon, and (this being Becca) manages to flirt with a couple of guys.

When she walks away, I even overhear a guy ask his buddy, "Is it me, or did Eager Beaver somehow get hot?" I'll make sure to tell her later.

When it's almost time for Becca and me to trade places, I signal Melanie and plan B begins.

Melanie walks by and says hi to both

me and Crystal and then does a double take when she sees Alex.

"Oh, my God," she says with Oscar-worthy conviction. "Aren't you Alex Walker?"

Alex looks confused. Crystal looks angry.

"Do I know you?" he asks.

"I'm Melanie White. From Camp Minnagawa."

Alex once mentioned a summer camp that he went to back when he was in middle school. Melanie spent half the night researching it online.

"You were at Camp Minnagawa?"

Melanie raises her hand in salute. "Camp Minnagawa. Where little acorns—"

"Become mighty oaks," he finishes. "Oh, my God. What a small world."

He gives her another hard look, and she keeps playing it perfectly.

"Mel White."

He smiles. "That's right. I remember you."

Bingo.

"That's incredible that you guys know each other," I say, smiling.

"Yeah," Crystal adds with a hint of sarcasm. "Incredible."

"Stupid me," I say, slapping my head.

"What?" Alex says.

"I forgot. I'm supposed to go help my dad on the fire truck."

"Do you want me to go with you?" Alex asks.

"No, it's fine," I assure him. "Stay here."

"Absolutely," Melanie says. "We've got lots to catch up on."

She winks, and I make my exit. Crystal is about to pop an eyelid or something. Alex is completely convinced that he and Melanie have known each other for years.

Becca and I meet up inside the Magic Waters minivan. It's kind of a tight spot to change, but we don't have a lot of choice.

"I cannot believe how hot it is in this thing," Becca says as she wriggles out of the costume.

"You were awesome, Bec. Absolutely awesome."

"Did you like the part when I gave Crystal a get-well hug?"

"It was brilliant."

I start to get dressed. I hope it's dark enough so that nobody can see into the van.

"How's Melanie doing?"

I can't help but laugh. "She's got it totally under control. By the time she's done, he'll be convinced that they were sweethearts back in fifth grade."

I'm almost all the way dressed when Becca stops cold and says something that catches me completely off guard.

"I hope this guy is worth all this trouble." She's not being sarcastic or mean-spirited. She's being honest. "Because personally, I don't think any guy is."

"Then why are you doing it?" I ask.

She shakes her head. "Because I do think that *you're* worth it. You'd better go dance your little beaver tail off."

"Thanks, Becca."

I jump out of the van and rush over to an area behind the band shell where Grayson is waiting to go on.

He shoots me a *Where were you?* look.

"Sorry. Had to pee."

Just then it's time for us to run onstage. I think to myself that I may actually be able to pull this off. Then I put on my giant beaver head and everything goes wrong.

I had adjusted the helmet to fit Becca

so that she could see out of the eye slits. But I forgot to put it back for me. As I walk out onto the stage I realize that I can't see a thing. I am completely blind. The music starts, and I try to do the dance by memory.

"*Platypus Rex and Eager Beaver*
Our furry water friends
Want you to be a believer
In making pollution end . . ."

There are scattered laughs and I'm not sure if they're normal or if it's because I'm pointing in the wrong direction or something.

"*You've got to keep our magic waters*
Crystal blue and clear
So that we can save the Otters
Like our good friend here . . ."

This is the cue for Ollie Otter to walk onstage. The problem is that our stage at Magic Waters is bigger. We're a little more crowded here and the girl in the costume has to walk right next to me.

I do a spin and slam into her.

This starts a horrifying chain reaction that knocks Ollie to the ground and sends me hurtling into the crowd. I try to catch myself, but it's no use. I hit the ground with a big thump, and then the unthinkable happens.

My head falls off.

Well, not my head. But Eager Beaver's head falls off. Needless to say, it's pretty traumatic for the hundred or so children in the crowd.

There are shrieks and screams, and the image of Eager Beaver's head rolling across the stage will undoubtedly work its way into nightmares for years to come.

I have my own little nightmare image. It's Alex looking right at me, trying to make sense of it all.

I grab Eager Beaver's head and put it on as quickly as possible. But it's too late. Although I'm still blind, I manage to stumble my way through to the end of the dance.

By the time I get back into my street clothes, Alex is long gone. No doubt Crystal was more than happy to fill him in on any details he couldn't figure out for himself.

Twenty-five

As fireworks fill the sky, I'm where I've been every Fourth of July that I can remember: I'm wading through the surf side by side with Becca and Melanie.

No one really says much for a while. We just watch the pinwheels and sparklers light up the sky and listen to them rumble. Finally, Becca breaks the ice.

"I just want to say that although Operation Busy Beaver was not technically a success, I thought it went pretty well."

I give her a look. "Did you hear those poor children when they thought Eager Beaver was dead?"

"Well, not that part."

"What about the part where Crystal took Alex and disappeared?"

"Yeah. But you're focusing on all the bad stuff."

"Tell me a part that went well."

"How about Melanie pulling off the whole Camp Minnagawa thing? You know how shy she is. She nailed that baby. She was Middle School Camp Girl."

Melanie smiles, and I have to agree with Becca's analysis.

"And Becca was some kind of Eager Beaver," Melanie says. "All warm and cuddly. Just like she isn't in real life."

We all laugh.

"You're right," I say. "You two were brilliant. I was the one who dropped the ball."

Bec throws an arm around me. "Things happen that you can't control. But you didn't drop the ball. You got the ball rolling."

Melanie laughs. "You got that head rolling too."

I stop and think back on the evening.

"What am I going to do, guys?"

"You mean about Alex?"

I shake my head. "No. About me. I've been something of a madwoman lately."

Becca smiles. "You know, in health class they taught us about those two-step programs. Maybe you need to do something like that."

Melanie gives her a look. "They're not two-step programs. The two-step's a dance. They're twelve-step programs."

Becca laughs. "You think I pay attention in health class? I can only remember two."

"What are they?" I ask her.

"First you have to admit you have a problem," Melanie says.

"Well, I'm happy to do that." I stop and yell out at the top of my lungs, "I am a madwoman." The sound is mostly drowned out by the fireworks, although some people turn to look.

"What's the other step?"

"Apologizing to the people your insanity affected."

This one hits home. This is what I must do.

"You're right," I say. "That's perfect. I need to apologize. And let me start with you two. I am so sorry."

Melanie laughs. "Are you crazy? I

haven't had this much fun in a long time."

"Ditto," Becca adds.

I stop and give each of them a bear hug.

"Ouch," Becca says. "My boobs are still recovering from the beaver suit."

Later that night I wander into my house to find my father in the kitchen. He's obviously been waiting for me.

"Hey, Daddy."

"Hey, Jane. I thought you might need this."

He reaches into the freezer and pulls out a pint of Chunky Monkey. I smile and give him a big hug. For the first time, slight tears start to fall along my cheek.

"Thanks, Dad."

"It's nothing to lose your head over."

"Dad! That's not funny."

We go into the family room, and he stops his comedy routine for a moment.

"You know who I was thinking about right before you got home?" he asks.

I shake my head.

"Melanie's mom, Judi." He pauses for a moment. "You know, she would have laughed so hard when your beaver head fell off. I can hear it in my head. She would have thought that was hilarious."

For the first time in hours, I smile. Dad's absolutely right: Mrs. White had a great sense of humor and a loud laugh that filled any room.

We channel surf until we find *Bring It On*. He spends half an hour trying to convince me that what seems like a movie about cheerleaders is actually all about the fall of Communism.

I hardly see the movie. Instead, I keep replaying the night over in my head. I see Becca dressed up as Eager Beaver and Melanie pretending to be a girl from camp. It's like I'm watching it all on DVD. Except, when I get to the worst part, there is no pause or stop button.

I picture Eager Beaver's head rolling across the stage and I can fully see Alex's reaction. There's only one way I can stop it.

I have to go see Alex first thing in the morning.

Twenty-six

The drive out to Alex's house is almost unbearable. I really don't know what I'm going to say to him. I don't even know if he'll talk to me. I leave the stereo off the whole way. I'm not really in the mood to deal with Radio Karma right now.

I walk up to the door and just stand there for a moment, trying to collect my thoughts. That's when I hear the voice.

"Are you going to knock or are you just going to stand there?"

It's Alex. He's caught me at the door again.

"That depends," I say as I take a deep breath. "Do you want me to come in or do you never want to see me again?"

He looks me over for a moment and then does his crooked little smile. "Come on, let's talk."

We go inside, and I take a quick look around, making sure that Josie is nowhere to be seen.

"Don't worry," he says. "She's gone."

"About last night," I blurt out.

He holds up his hands. "Before we talk about that, I need to tell you something." He pauses, trying to find the right words.

"What is it?" I ask.

Finally, he gets it out. "We're not going to be able to keep seeing each other."

Even though I knew it was coming, it knocks the wind right out of me. I really don't want to cry in front of him, but a few tears start to fall anyway.

"I understand," I say, clearing my throat. "And I really can't blame you."

He gives me a confused look. "Why do you say that?"

"Because of, you know . . . last night and everything that happened."

"No, it's not that."

"Then what is it?"

"It's my father."

Now I'm really confused.

He moves over and sits right next to me. "My dad has to go to London to handle some big case, and Josie's going with him. So I'm going to spend the rest of summer back home with my mom. She's finished her documentary early. I'm going to fly to Washington . . . tomorrow."

Now the waterworks really begin.

"So it's not because of the whole mermaid-beaver thing?"

He smiles. "Not at all. That was a little . . . weird. But it was also kind of cute."

"I'm so sorry that I lied to you."

He smiles and cracks a little laugh and then he wraps me up in a big hug. "It's not like it was a big lie," he says. "I just don't understand why you went to all the trouble."

Funny. It made so much sense at the time.

"I thought you'd think I was a dork if you knew I was a giant beaver. Mermaid just sounded . . . sexier."

"Personally, I think the beaver costume is pretty sexy. But that's just me."

He smiles, and I laugh. But it's this really kind of repulsive laugh because I'm crying and my nose is congested. I'm a total wreck.

He puts his arms around me, and I cry against his chest. "This is what I was worried about that night up in the lifeguard stand," he says as he strokes my hair. "I'm so sorry, baby."

The "baby" is what really does me in. It just sounds so *right*. I slobber all over his shirt for a while, and he doesn't rush me. He just keeps stroking my hair.

After about a minute or so, he asks, "Want to watch a movie? I know a theater that's already open."

I sit up and try to compose myself. "Sure."

"First, though, I'd better change my shirt."

I look down and I'm horrified to see that I have goobered all over his shirt. I don't even know if dry cleaning could take care of it.

"Sorry," I say.

"It's okay."

He does a quick change, and we head upstairs to the home theater. He does his best to keep the mood light, and I do my best to act like I'm not going to cry for the rest of my life.

"You'll be happy to know that I have found something other than *Blue Crush* for us to watch," he says as he sorts through the DVDs.

"Too bad," I say. "I can never get enough of that movie. What'd you find instead?"

"*The Princess Bride*," he says. "Have you ever seen it?"

I shake my head. "I've never even heard of it."

"Trust me. You'll love it."

He's right about the movie. It really is good. It's funny and it's romantic. And it believes in sappy things like true love. We watch the whole thing leaning against each other with his arm around me.

When the movie ends, we start to hook up on the couch. But a few minutes later that ends when we hear the front door open. It's Josie back from some sort of collagen injection or something.

"Hello," she calls out in her nightmare nasal voice. "I'm home."

"Up here," he calls out.

"I hate to say this, but I have to get to work," he tells me.

I nod. "Me too."

We walk down the stairs and find Josie in unbelievably inappropriate workout clothes. I cough to keep from laughing.

"Janet!" she says like we're old friends.

"It's Jane," Alex says.

"Of course, Jane," she says. "I'm so sorry. Listen, girlfriend, I'm about to do Pilates. If you're dope with that, you could join me."

Now it's getting hard not to laugh. "I'm *dope* with it. But I've really got to get to work."

She nods knowingly. "I'm down with that." (Which is funny, because Alex told me she's never worked a single day in her life.)

Luckily Alex comes to my rescue. "You'd better get to your car."

"A-ight, then," Josie says. "Next time you're in the 'hood, just holla."

"I'll definitely do that," I say as we leave.

We hold hands as we walk to my car.

"Wait right here," he says. "There's something I need to get out of my car."

He walks over and pops his trunk and pulls out a present. It's wrapped in red paper with a big gold bow.

"I was going to bring it over to your house before I went to work."

I open it and smile. It's a big bulky USC sweatshirt.

"I ordered it online," he says. "I want you to have it so you can remember why you're training so hard. That swim team doesn't know how lucky they are."

"Keep my eyes on the prize," I say, quoting Becca.

"Exactly."

"I love it," I tell him. "It's really great."

I feel like I'm about to cry again, and I really don't want to do that. I catch it and clear my throat.

"I brought something for you, too." I lean into the backseat and pull out a large manila envelope. "It's your swim certificate."

He lights up as he opens it. I did it in Photoshop, and I think it turned out pretty good.

He reads off of the certificate: "'For

battling demons of the deep—both real and imagined, Alexander Walker has achieved the rank of Grand Pollywog.'

"It's absolutely perfect," he says.

"You should be proud, Alex. It's not easy to overcome your fears. Believe me, I know that."

He reads it again to himself, and I see that wonderful smile one last time.

"I can't believe I'm so excited about being a stupid Pollywog," he says.

I look at him and smile too. "I don't know. I think Pollywog's pretty sexy. But maybe that's just me."

He wraps me in a huge hug, and we kiss.

It's funny how you remember things. The thing I remember about our kiss up on the lifeguard stand is the taste of the salt in the air. And the thing I remember about our first kiss in the pool is the taste of the chlorine.

This last kiss I'll remember for its taste too.

It's the taste of tears sliding down onto our lips. But the amazing thing is that the tears aren't mine.

They're his.

Twenty-seven

"Jane . . . Jane."

I snap out of my daze and look up to see Grayson with a concerned look on his face. "You're still talking to me?" I say with a smile.

He nods and sits down across the table from me. "I'm still talking to you." The look of concern returns to his face. "Are you okay?"

Not an easy question. I'm still digesting the fact that Alex is leaving. I'd expected him to dump me, but the leaving has caught me off guard. I figure that I might as well be honest. "I've got a little bit of a broken heart."

"I'm sorry to hear that," he says.

"It was kind of self-inflicted," I say. "But I'll be okay."

We just sit there for a while, not saying much of anything.

"I really want to apologize," I tell him. "For everything. You've been great to me. You've helped me so much. And I got you sucked up into the whole mess. I'm really sorry."

"I don't think you have anything to be sorry about," he says. "But if it helps, your apology is accepted."

"It helps a lot."

"You should look on the bright side," he says.

"There's a bright side?"

"At least you don't have to tell the SAT fart story the next time someone asks about your most embarrassing moment."

This makes me laugh.

"I was at both," he continues. "And believe me, the Fourth of July was much more embarrassing."

"That's true," I say. "You were at both."

"I must be your ultimate bad-luck charm."

I think about this for a moment. "I don't think that's it. I think you're good luck. We've just had bad timing."

"You know what they say. 'Timing is everything.'"

I look over and see Crystal headed into the locker room. Our paths are constantly crossing, and I keep trying to avoid her.

"You're right," I say. "Timing *is* everything."

I get up and go straight to the locker room. That's where I find her.

"Crystal, can I talk to you for a second?"

She rolls her eyes and gives her friends a look. "I guess so. What is it?"

"It's private."

I don't wither or give in. I just stand there and wait until she signals her friends to move along.

"Fine. We're *private*. What's the big deal?"

"I just wanted to say I'm sorry."

This catches her completely off guard.

"It may not matter to you. And you may not deserve it. But I *am* sorry."

She just gives me a totally glazed-over look and says, "Whatever." Then she starts

230

to walk away. It gets under my skin, and suddenly I feel like addressing three years' worth of unfinished business.

I walk around and get right in her face. "What is your problem?"

"I don't have any problems."

"I think you do," I tell her.

"Why is that? Because I'm popular and you're not? Or because I have boyfriends and you don't? Or maybe it's that I don't hang around with everyone like we were still back in Girl Scouts?"

It's all coming out.

"You know something? Those things do hurt. They really do. Especially being friends. We were good friends—all four of us—and you just dumped us. That hurt me. It hurt Becca. And it hurt Melanie. But I understand that. I understand that you had a chance to be something that I didn't and you made a choice to be that way. Believe me. I've gotten over it."

"Then what's *your* problem?"

She looks at me, and I can't read her. But it doesn't matter. This is the plus side of Bikini Jane—confidence. I'm going to tell her off.

"You're my problem. Think about all of those times that we had sleepovers at Melanie's house. All the times that Mrs. White stayed up with us and drove us to movies and took us to the beach. Think about all of those times that she treated us like we were all her daughters. And you didn't even have the decency to show up at her funeral.

"That's when I decided to hate you, Crystal. That's the moment I decided that you really are a bitch!"

I just stand there. I have finally gotten it off of my chest and I am ready for whatever she sends back at me. But when I look at her, I'm amazed by what I see. She is actually crying. Not just little drops, but a steady stream of tears rolling down her face.

She tries to say something, but she can't. Her mouth and nose are all clogged up. Finally, she clears her throat.

"I was there. I was at the funeral and the cemetery."

"That's funny, because I didn't see you. And neither did Melanie."

"I didn't want you to see me. I stood far away so that you wouldn't."

"Why?"

"I was embarrassed. I knew you all hated me. And I thought you wouldn't want to see me. I thought avoiding you was the least I could do."

It hits me that she's being sincere. "Maybe you should try to do a little more than that sometimes."

"How?"

"You could talk to Melanie. As far as she's concerned, there are only three people her age who will ever know what her mom was like—Becca, me, and you."

She continues crying, and for once, I actually believe they're real tears. Even though it's against my will, I hug her, and she buries her face in my shoulder.

While she's crying, I look in the locker room mirror and see what I've become.

I'm not Plain Jane.

I'm not Bikini Jane.

Finally, I'm just Jane.

Twenty-eight

The last month of summer unfolds rather uneventfully. Which is a good thing. I do my best to keep the maniac behavior to a minimum. I spend a lot more time training in the pool and a lot less time obsessing over guys. (Don't get me wrong. We still go to parties and enjoy the eye candy.) I also settle in to giving swim lessons to short, chunky kids and not tall, hunky guys. And I make sure to keep my Wednesdays open so that Mel and I can keep up with all the action on *Smallville* and *American Idol*.

Believe it or not, by the last day of summer, I'm ready to start school again.

Well, almost. I do have big plans for that last day. It starts in the morning, when I insist on making the cereal for Mom and Dad.

"I think she's up to something," Dad says. "Why's she making the cereal?"

"You're right, Dad. I'm trying to *hood-wink* you."

Mom and I both laugh.

"Laugh all you want," Dad says. "That word's making a comeback."

The truth is, I am setting them up. I stop and reach into the cereal. "Wait a second," I say. "What's this?"

"What is it?" my dad says.

"It's . . . a check," I say, pulling it out of the box. "A check for $1,250." I grin from ear to ear as I hand it to them. "Thanks for the car."

For once, my dad is speechless.

Late that afternoon, I head over to Mama Taco's to hook up with Becca and Melanie. When I get there, Bec meets me at the door.

"Check it out." She motions across the room, and I see something that I never imagined I'd see again. Melanie and

Crystal are sharing a booth. Crystal is telling some story, and Mel is completely wrapped up in it. When she reaches the end, they both laugh.

I give Bec a *What the hell?* look.

"It's been going on for over an hour."

If I didn't see it, I wouldn't believe it. "What are they talking about?"

"Mel's mom. All the old stories. Like the one when she went with us to TP Trish Bartholomew's house. She didn't want us to get in trouble, but she ended up being the one who got chased by the cops."

I laugh just thinking about it. It was the highlight of eighth grade. "She sure was fast."

I look at them and suddenly miss the old days. The four of us. "Should we go over and join them?"

Becca shakes her head. "No. Melanie needs this."

"You're right. Let's go sit on the patio."

We go out to the patio and get a table.

Becca and I slowly make our way through a basket of chips and guac as we enjoy the view and the cool ocean breeze.

"So the Summer of Love is coming to an end."

I nod. "One more day and we'll be seniors."

Becca flashes a wicked smile. "God save Ruby Beach High School."

I look across the patio toward the ocean and see a pleasant surprise. It's Grayson. He approaches us, although he seems a bit nervous.

"Hi, Jane. Hi, Becca."

"Grab a seat."

He sits down with us. He takes a deep breath and turns to Becca. "I'm sorry, but do you think Jane and I could be alone for a second?"

Becca smiles, and I have no idea what's going on. "Absolutely," she says as she gets up to walk away. But first, she turns back around and talks to Grayson. "By the way," she says, "Melanie and I were rooting for you all summer long."

She holds the smile a second more and leaves.

Slowly, I'm beginning to figure this out.

"I'm not . . . really . . . good at this,"

Grayson stammers. "I mean, that's probably pretty obvious since I went the entire summer without saying anything."

I think back to when Melanie told me that she was certain Grayson liked me. Maybe she was right.

"Grayson, what do you want to tell me?"

He takes a deep breath. "That . . . I like you. That I've always liked you."

What do you know? Melanie was right. But somehow I'm still caught off guard, and I feel butterflies in my stomach. "Why didn't you say anything?"

He fidgets for a moment. It is the most vulnerable I've ever seen him. It's really quite charming.

"You were kind of busy," he stammers. "You know—with Mr. Gorgeous."

It's kind of funny that he calls Alex "Mr. Gorgeous." I mean, it's true and all. But he's been gone for over a month.

"What about after he left? Why didn't you tell me then?"

"I started to, a couple of times," he says. "But you seemed pretty heartbroken."

I look up at him and stare into his eyes. "And now?"

"It's the last day of summer," he says. "It's my last chance."

We both smile.

"Did you have anything in mind?" I ask him.

He nods. "I'd love it if you'd go out to dinner with me."

I play coy for a second before saying, "That would be great."

And there it is. I feel totally relaxed and excited at the same time.

This is how it's supposed to feel.

He smiles, and I do too. We look like a couple of goofballs. "Great. I made plans just in case you said that. Come with me. I've got a surprise."

In a few minutes we're driving along Ruby Beach Avenue and I'm getting kind of excited. The Summer of Love is coming down to the wire, but it's ending well.

Then he stops at Magic Waters.

"What are we doing here?" I ask in mock terror.

"Just follow me."

The park is dark and vacant with a sliver of moonlight cutting through the night sky.

He leads me around a corner, and suddenly we're at the mermaid lagoon. It's like nothing I've ever seen before. At night, the underwater lights give the water a magical blue sparkle. A picnic dinner has been set up along the rocks above. We're the only ones there, and it's beautiful.

"How'd you do this?"

"I've been here for three years," he says. "Some people owe me favors."

I've been to Magic Waters more times than I can ever count. But I've never once thought it was pretty. At least not until now. "It's perfect."

"I thought you might like to try it out."

"Try what out?"

"Being a mermaid," he says. "Isn't that what you wanted all summer long?"

I look out at the lagoon and realize that he's absolutely right.

"I don't have a suit."

"I'll avert my eyes," he says as he covers them with his hands. After a second, two of the fingers spread apart enough so he can still peek. I don't care. I strip down to my bra and a pair of boy shorts, and for some reason I don't feel the least bit self-conscious.

I dive in and swim all the way to the bottom. I go all around the pool, just like I thought I was going to do before the summer began. When I break the surface I float on my back for a moment, the water lapping across my body. I look up and all I see are the moon and stars.

I glance over and I see Grayson placing a boom box on the picnic blanket.

"One last thing," he says. "Radio Karma."

I tread water for a moment. "Okay. Turn it on."

The music starts, and I laugh. "How did you do that?"

"Do what?"

"How did you make that song come on?" I ask.

He smiles. "It wasn't me. It was the music gods." I don't know if I believe him or not. I want to. Because the song's perfect. Corny, but perfect. It's John Mayer, and he's singing love and bodies pressed against each other.

Suddenly, I want to be close to him. I swim to the edge where he is standing and I reach up. "Help me out."

As he goes to give me a hand, I pull

him right in, clothes and all. Soon we're both laughing and splashing each other.

"Try to keep up," I say as I swim away to the waterfall. When he gets there, I grab him. It's there in the falling water that we kiss for the first time.

I kiss him like I've never kissed anyone in my entire life, and he does the same right back. It's not like the movies. It's wet and sloppy, and I keep my eyes open the whole time because I don't want to miss a thing.

Epilogue

I used to think that my life was a conspiracy. That everyone in the world was working against me. It's funny, but it's easier to think that your problems are caused by 4 billion people you don't know than it is to admit that they're your own doing. You make them. You can solve them. It took my pretending to be somebody else to figure out who I really am.

Realizing this is coming in handy as I try to adjust to life as a senior. I have one more year before I'll leave for college. I hope I'll have it all figured out by then.

Right now, though, I'm not trying to figure out anything. I'm just sitting back

...d enjoying the first football game of the year. From my seat here on the top row of Bobcat Stadium, I can see most everything that's important to me.

My dad is sitting beyond the end zone in the back of an ambulance. He's there in case anybody gets hurt, and I'm certain he's passing the time by telling his partner bad jokes or trying to convince him how some Lindsay Lohan movie holds the secrets to understanding the universe.

Mom is working in the concession booth with the rest of the English department. She carries herself so well that she even makes working the cotton candy machine seem classy.

Crystal was elected captain of the cheerleading squad. (Big shocker there.) Just as she will certainly be elected Homecoming Princess and Prom Queen. She's still my nemesis, and I still don't like her. But she smiles more and backstabs less. Sometimes, she even has lunch alone with Melanie, which means there really is a person beneath all that plastic surgery.

Melanie's sitting right next to me shouting her head off and wearing a letterman's jacket. It's Kevin Cavanaugh's. He may not know how to spell "sexy," but at least he was smart enough to ask Mel to tutor him for the SAT. Two weeks later, they became a couple and picked up where they left off at the Pirates of the Caribbean so many years ago.

Normally, Becca would sit with us and dish about the cheerleaders and how hideous their uniforms are. But, now, she's actually on the field. Apparently her time in the Eager Beaver costume made quite an impression. She's now dressed in the furry costume of Crazy Cat—mascot for the Ruby Beach Bobcats. This way she can show the school spirit that she's always secretly had and she can still maintain her cool, aloof persona. (I swear to god, I overheard a senior say, "Is it me or is Crazy Cat kind of hot?")

I can't see Alex, but I am wearing the USC sweatshirt he gave me. He e-mails a lot and has even called a couple times. He will always be someone really special to me. He'll always be the first guy I ever fell in love with. And, even though there was a lot of embarrassment, that will always be great.

Sometimes I wonder what would have happened if he hadn't left Florida. I don't know if we would have stayed together, but in my heart, I don't think so. I think it lasted the right amount of time. For a long-term relationship, I think you need to be more comfortable. More at ease.

Which is exactly how I feel with Grayson. Right now, my eyes are glued to number 14 on the other side of the field. He's the kicker for the Fletcher Senators, but I knew him first as a dancing platypus.

He's also my boyfriend.

It's not going to be easy. He's at a different school and our lives are spread apart, but that night in the mermaid lagoon was only the beginning. So far, it's been great. He's sweet and funny and sexy, and even mushy. Sometimes he even manages to sneak love notes into my locker at school. (I suspect Melanie is his accomplice, but neither one is talking.)

Where's it heading? How serious will it get?

Those are good questions.

I think back to that party and when he told us that guys are much more willing to accept "I don't know" as an answer.

Maybe they're onto something. Because I don't know the answers.

And I'm more than okay with that.

About the Author

Jamie Ponti grew up in Atlantic Beach, Florida—a town that bears a striking resemblance to Ruby Beach—but refuses to reveal the true identities of who ran over whose foot, who actually mistook a bidet for a water fountain, or what inspired *el lollipop del amor*.

Like the main character in this book, Jamie worked in a theme park and went to the University of Southern California, but was in fact a terrible swimmer who flunked out of Pollywog class.

In addition to *Animal Attraction*, Jamie has written and produced television shows for Nickelodeon, the Disney Channel, PBS, the History Channel, and Spike TV.

When I got to the Book Nook, I spotted
Audre sitting on a plump sofa in the back,
pretending to knit a scarf. What she was
really doing, of course, was checking out
Griffin McCarthy, the hottie who works at
the register.

Audre and I are obsessed with the Book
Nook, and not only because of Griffin. It's
this adorable bookstore that's right
between our houses. In the front, where I
was wringing the rain out of my low ponytail, are rows of shelves spilling over with
books. The owner's ink-black cats, who are
all named after famous authors, roam
around on the bright orange-and-blue
rugs. In the back is a small café full of
squishy chairs and couches where people
sip vanilla cappuccinos and click away on
their laptops. Actual writers hang there; I

always hoped I would run into Philippa Askance, this punk poetess I worship, but I hadn't yet. The air smells of fresh coffee beans and the best music is always playing in the background. Today, the Pixies were serenading us.

"You survived," Audre said as I plopped down beside her. She moved her knitting drumsticks and tangle of yellow yarn aside, then pecked my cheek.

"You changed," I said, gesturing to her outfit.

To school that day, Audre had worn skinny cords, a purple cowl-neck, and her leopard-print flats. Now she was wearing an off-the-shoulder striped shirt and denim mini over fishnets and fuzzy boots. Her hair was pulled back in a curly dark poof, big gold hoops dangled from her ears, and the shimmery blush on her cheekbones turned her cocoa-colored skin all glowy. It was obvious she'd made the special effort for Griffin. He doesn't work at the Book Nook every afternoon, but Audre has his schedule tacked up on the wall in her bedroom so she knows when she'll see him.

I'm serious.

"What's your point?" Audre grinned as she ran her pinkie over her full, glossy bottom lip.

"That you did *not* come here to knit," I teased. "Have you talked to him yet?" I turned to look at the register, where I'd seen Griffin a second before. Another guy was now in his place, so I glanced back toward the coffee counter, where a tattooed girl was tending to some customers. "Hey, Aud, where'd your loverboy go—"

"Norah, Audre. What's up?" There was no mistaking that deep, slow-as-honey voice. I looked behind me, feeling my cheeks redden. There stood the loverboy in question, holding two steaming mugs and smiling at us from under his mop of shaggy golden hair.

"Griffin!" Audre and I exclaimed at the same instant, then looked at each other and burst into giggles.

Hello, mortification. My name is Norah. Perhaps we've met before?

Griffin didn't seem to notice our girly reaction. He simply set the mugs on the table in front of us, and stretched his six-foot surfer's frame into a chair across from us.

"Two lattes, extra foam. Am I right?" he asked, winking at Audre as he toyed with the shell choker around his neck. Griffin isn't really my type—the blond California thing doesn't do it for me—but he's definitely cute and, like all boys, totally ties my tongue. It doesn't help that he's a freshman at New York University, so I'm forever wanting to pump him for the inside scoop on college—but I'm usually too nervous. I figure he wouldn't bother giving advice to a random high school junior.

"Well, we come here enough," Audre replied, cool as ever. She is forever poised, even in front of boys she likes. I watched as she lifted one of the mugs and took a long sip, then closed her eyes and tipped her head to one side, getting into what I call her Gourmet Diva Mode. "Mmm. Hazelnut infusion," she said approvingly.

I sipped at the hot, foamy drink. All I tasted was milk and coffee. But that is the difference between Audre and me. Or, actually, between Audre and most high school kids. My best friend already has her life pretty much mapped out: She wants to go to cooking school and become a total domestic goddess, with her own line of pastry cookbooks and a television show: the African-American Nigella Lawson. Meanwhile, I have no idea what I want out of the future—except college. And now even that seemed like a giant question mark.

"*Gracias.*" Griffin shot Audre a slow grin. "Just brewed 'em myself." The tattooed girl from the coffee counter wiggled past Griffin on her way to the front of the store, and I noticed that he followed her with his eyes.

"Aren't you supposed to work the register?" Audre asked, fluttering her lashes at him. It kills me that my best friend knows how to flirt without ever, to my knowledge, having taken any lessons.

"I've got a sweet deal with Patrick," Griffin replied. "When one of us has friends come in, the other one covers the register."

I snuck a peek at Audre, knowing she was loving that Griffin had called us his friends. She was trying not to smile, but her deep dimples gave her away. I grinned too.

Griffin was the social butterfly of the Book Nook, chatting up everyone from hipster writers to paint-stained artists. And his NYU buddies—most of them crush-worthy, floppy-haired types—would sometimes drop by for free coffee. It *was* kind of flattering to be included in that circle, and I felt a sudden rush of confidence. If Griffin considered me a friend, there was no harm in asking him a few questions about getting into college. Maybe he would put my mind at ease after the Ms. Bliss fiasco.

I cleared my throat and took off my glasses. "Griffin?" I began. "Did you, um, when you applied to NYU, did you do lots of—"

"Drugs?" Griffin cut me off, his hazel eyes twinkling. He lazily rubbed a hand across the front of his worn blue T-shirt. "Dude, I must have been smoking *something* because NYU is so not the right school for me."

"It's not?" Audre set down her latte with a frown, most likely tortured by visions of Griffin transferring to another city.

Griffin sighed. "It's a dope place and all, but these New York winters bring me down. Back in Santa Monica, I'd hit the beach with my friends every afternoon. I know it's messed up, but sometimes I miss high school. You know?"

Audre and I glanced at each other in horrified disbelief.

"You. Are. Crazy," Audre pronounced, staring at Griffin as if he'd just sprouted another gorgeous head.

"Don't get us started on high school," I jumped in, forgetting my nervousness. "Especially *today*. They played these disgusting love songs like 'I Wanna Be with You' over the P.A. system during lunch and—"

"Our English teacher made us watch that lame *Romeo and Juliet* movie—not even the Claire and Leo one," Audre groaned, rolling her eyes. I nodded emphatically. Audre and I have been finishing each other's sentences since we met in the Prospect Park playground at age four. Griffin watched us with a small smirk, clearly amused.

"Not like English class doesn't suck on regular days," I added, and pointed to the stack of shiny paperbacks on the table in front of us. "I mean, there are so many incredible books in the world, and we're stuck reading dull, creepy stuff like *Heart of Darkness*." English was a sore point for me; it's usually my favorite subject, but our teacher this year, Mr. Whitmore, was a white-bearded snooze who sucked all the juiciness out of literature and droned on about grammar.

Griffin chuckled and ran a hand through his blond hair. "Dude, I hate to break it to you, but you still get assigned boring reading in college." Then his face lit up as he leaned forward. "Though you know what some of my friends have been into lately? Book groups."

"Book groups?" I echoed, feeling a pin-prick of curiosity.

"As in, like, Oprah?" Audre asked dubiously.

"But more fun," Griffin replied. "Just some friends getting together over beers once a month to chill and talk about, like, *On the Road*. It's cool 'cause *you* get to pick the books, not some stodgy teacher."

Hmm. Book groups. I pictured Audre, Scott, and myself hanging out in Audre's bedroom, drinking ciders that her older brother bought for us and debating the new Louise Rennison novel. True, Audre and Scott don't love to read as much as I do, and we *were* swamped with school and SAT prep. Plus, Audre had her baking class, while Scott juggled Art Club, Student Council, and a zillion other extracurriculars—

Wait. That was *it*! I almost spilled my latte as I sat bolt upright. *Start your own club*, Ms. Bliss had said. A book group would count as a real activity, wouldn't it? I'd need a teacher's permission to make it official, but any sane adult would okay a club that was all about reading. And talk about showing colleges commitment *and* initiative. Take that, Ms. Bliss!

"Who's Ms. Bliss?" Griffin asked.

Oh, God. My cheeks burned and I quickly drank more of my latte, hoping to disappear behind the giant mug. Had I spoken those last words *out loud*? One snicker from Audre confirmed my suspicion.

"Our guidance counselor," she explained casually. Then she elbowed me in the ribs. "And, Nors, I know what you're thinking, and the answer is a resounding 'no.'"

"Good for you, Psychic Hotline," I snapped, annoyed that she was so quick to burst my bubble. "So what if I want to start a book group? You're saying you won't join?" That *couldn't* happen; I suck at organizing anything so I'd need both Audre and Scott's support to get a club off the ground.

Audre crossed her arms over her chest in her favorite you-are-not-changing-my-mind pose. "It'd be like having more homework."

"Not if you read good stuff," Griffin pointed out. He eased up out of the chair and stretched his arms above his head, giving us a delicious glimpse of his bare olive stomach. "And, hey, you could even hold your meetings here. I'd be happy to bring you guys drinks. "

Aha! This time, without even looking at Audre, I knew her dimples were showing. If anything was going to convince my stubborn best friend to take part in the group, it would be the chance to see more of her crush.

"I gotta hit the register before my boss finds me," the object of Audre's affection announced. "Norah, keep me posted 'bout this book group gig. I don't have time to join, but a friend of mine might be interested." When he looked my way, he grinned. Then, without warning, he strolled right up to me, crouched low, and leaned in toward my face.

I froze, and then flushed all over. What was going on? Was Griffin going to kiss me? My very first kiss—here, in the Book Nook? Would Audre get mad? Thank God I'd taken off my glasses, but I wished I'd at least put some Burt's Beeswax balm on my lips—

"Foam," Griffin said, wiping my upper

lip with his warm thumb. "A danger of latte-drinking." He winked, stood up, and shot Audre a quick salute. "Later, ladies."

We sat there in stunned silence for several seconds. Finally, I managed to turn to Audre and say, "He so likes you."

"Whatever," Audre replied. "He's a flirt. With me. With you. With everybody." She picked up a copy of *Fast Food Nation* from the table and thumbed through it. "Of course, that doesn't mean I'd be opposed to him serving me drinks. . . ." She glanced at me, her light brown eyes dancing.

Still shaky from the fake-out kiss, I barely dared believe my good luck. "The book group?" I whispered. "You mean you'll do it, Aud?" Quickly, I told her about my face-off with Ms. Bliss and how starting the group could be my last hope.

"If it'll help you with college stuff, I'm there," Audre said firmly when I was finished. She squeezed my arm. "Consider me your second-in-command. I can even provide the snacks." Then she grinned wickedly. "And maybe that friend Griffin mentioned can provide the extra eye-candy."

My heart fluttered for an instant. Would one of Griffin's NYU friends really join? That would be a nice bonus. I hadn't considered that, in addition to scoring me points with Ms. Bliss, this new club might improve my love life.

But, no. Good books *and* cute boys all at once?

While I was still in high school?

Not possible.

They just can't wait till graduation.

Mandy, Kai, Debbie, and Eva have one thing they must do before the end of high school . . . win the prestigious Treemont scholarship. It's a free pass to the college of their choice. But the award has one very bizarre little requirement: "Purity of soul and body."

In an effort to proclaim their "purity" to the whole school, Mandy starts the Virginity Club. The friends agree that a social service club is a great idea, but agreeing to keep the big V until graduation is another story. Because Mandy, Kai, Debbie, and Eva are each hiding something from the others. Something important.

And their secrets may cost them a whole lot more than just a scholarship. . . .

The Virginity Club

By Kate Brian, author of *The Princess & the Pauper*

PUBLISHED BY SIMON PULSE